MW00855729

OLD PROMISES

ETTIE SMITH AMISH MYSTERIES BOOK 15

SAMANTHA PRICE

AMISH SUSPENSE AND MYSTERY

Copyright © 2017 by Samantha Price
All rights reserved.

No part of this book may be reproduced in any form or by any
electronic or mechanical means, including information storage and
retrieval systems, without written permission from the author,
except for the use of brief quotations in a book review.

This book is a work of fiction. Any resemblance to any person,
living or dead, is purely coincidental. The personal names have been
invented by the author, and any likeness to the name of any person,
living or dead, is purely coincidental.

CHAPTER 1

"ETTIE, come away from the window. They might see you."

Ettie turned around and looked at her older sister, who was knitting as usual. "I'm just trying to get a glimpse of them. We need to see who's going to be living next door."

"They'll get the wrong impression if they see you staring out the window at them."

"It's okay, they can't see me. I said they wouldn't be Amish, and they aren't. I see a truck is there from the power company, and a man is running the wire for their electricity."

"I already told you two days ago that they wouldn't be Amish. Maize told me."

"I wouldn't rely on anything Maize said. Half the time she's talking about what happened twenty years ago."

"This time she was right." Elsa-May gave a sharp nod of her head, looking up briefly over the top of her thin-rimmed glasses. "I suppose there was a fifty-fifty probability either way. Since we have some Amish and some *Englisch* living on this road."

"I'm sure the new neighbors will be nice. All of the others have been lovely." Ettie kept watching the moving company men haul boxes into the house. Then, a smart-looking car pulled up behind the truck. "Hmm. Blue, or is it black, or gray?"

"For what?" Elsa-May said with noticeable exasperation.

Ettie chuckled. "They have a car. I'm trying to work out the color of it. It's an odd shade—that new metallic paintwork that changes color every time you change the angle you're looking from. There's a tall bald man getting out now, kind of heavy looking, and a smaller woman with dark wavy hair."

"How old are they?"

"Middle-aged, I'd say."

"Do they look nice?"

"Hard to tell. They're not talking or laughing, just walking toward the house."

Elsa-May continued clicking the knitting needles together as she spoke. "I just hope they don't see you staring. They'll think you're an old busybody."

Ettie pushed her lips out. "I just need to know who's going to be living beside us. There's nothing wrong with that, but what if they have an argument with us about the fence? It's getting old and we know it'll last another couple of years. They might want one right now and that would be a waste of money. If there's one thing I dislike it's—"

"Wasting money. I know. Why don't we do what everyone else does? Bake them a pie once they've moved in and take it over."

Ettie liked that idea. "What sort of pie?"

"Any kind. It doesn't matter. That's not the point."

"What if they don't like the pie?"

"Who cares?"

"I do. Everyone likes my pies. Maybe you should bake it and if they don't like it I can blame you." Ettie moved the curtains aside once more. "I want them to like me because then I can talk to them if they raise the issue of the fence."

"If that will shut you up then I'll bake the jolly pie."

Ettie tittered, then turned around and looked out the window once again. "Okay, *denke.*"

"Will you sit and rest a moment? It can't be that interesting watching the moving company people taking the furniture from the truck to the house."

"I saw them. I'm sure it was the new people. A man and a woman."

"Just sit," Elsa-May ordered.

"Very well." Ettie sat down, wondering why Elsa-May was so bothered. No one from outside could see her looking out the window. After a few minutes, a loud knock sounded on their door.

3

Elsa-May looked over the top of her glasses and dropped her knitting into her lap. "That'll be the new people now, Ettie."

"See, I should've stayed by the window then I wouldn't have had to get off the chair. It's so hard to get up these days."

"It saves me having to bake the pie." Elsa-May pushed her knitting back into the bag by her feet and Ettie got to the door ahead of her sister.

Ettie opened the door expecting to see their new neighbors. Instead, it was Myra, one of her estranged daughters. She'd lost weight, her cheeks were sunken and dark circles were etched under her eyes. Her hair was piled on top of her head and she wore a brightly-colored, flowing kaftan-style dress, much like the one she'd worn last time Ettie had seen her. From Myra's bothered expression, Ettie knew something was wrong.

"Mother, the police think I've killed someone."

Ettie gasped and looked around at Elsa-May. Elsa-May's jaw dropped open. Ettie looked back at Myra only to hear Elsa-May ask, "Did you do it?"

While Ettie grimaced at her sister, Myra pushed her way through the door seeming oblivious to her aunt's question. Myra sat heavily on the couch and Ettie hurried to sit by her.

"I was joking, Myra." Once Elsa-May was seated, Snowy lifted his head and made his way over to Myra.

"I apologize. I didn't think you could possibly be serious. Have you really been accused of murder?"

Myra gave a weak smile at her aunt as she leaned down to pat Snowy. "It's true. The police suspect me of murder, and it's not Myra anymore. I've changed my name."

"What to?" Ettie wondered what was wrong with the name her daughter had had all her life, the one her husband had particularly liked.

"I am now Sparkle Orient."

"What?" Ettie shrieked.

"She said—"

"I heard what she said, Elsa-May," Ettie snapped. "Why would you change your name, Myra?"

"It's 'Sparkle,'" Elsa-May corrected.

"I needed a new start. You see, it occurred to me that no one has a say in their own name and that seems wrong. How can you name a child when you don't know their personality?"

"Well, parents have got to call them something."

Myra patted Ettie's hand. "Don't worry. It's not your fault, and you're right. You and Father had to call me something. But I'm not a Myra now, I'm more of a Sparkle."

"What about Crowley, are you two still …?"

Ettie glared at her older sister. "Quiet, Elsa-May. I'm still trying to find out about the name."

"Didn't you two hear what I said? I've been accused of

murder. Who cares if Ronald and I are still together and why does everyone think a new name's such a big deal? If I get arrested and convicted, I could face life behind bars."

Elsa-May and Ettie looked at one another.

"I'm only here so you can make them see that I didn't do it, Mother. Isn't that what you do best?"

"Well … no."

"You haven't been charged with anything yet?" Elsa-May asked Myra.

"Not yet, but they think I did it. And Ronald is over-seas somewhere, so he's no help. I don't want him to find out about it either." Myra glared at them, each in turn, until they both nodded in agreement.

The way Myra looked sad when she talked about the former detective, Ronald Crowley, Ettie didn't feel like asking anything further about that. The pair were in a relationship of sorts, but since Myra was talking about a new start, maybe that meant she needed a new beginning because the relationship with Ronald hadn't worked out. Myra needed a decent man and Crowley was one, and he was in love with Myra. Ettie didn't think that would've changed. If they weren't together any longer, it would've been Myra who'd ended things.

"Why don't you start from the beginning, Sparkle?"

Ettie frowned at Elsa-May, at the way she'd adopted the new name without turning a hair.

"There's a client of mine who's been murdered. Ian Carter. You see, I'm a spiritual healer now. That's what I do for a living. The police think there was some highly toxic poison on the points of the healing crystals I gave Ian to take home."

Elsa-May leaned forward. "Did you say hearing crystals?"

"No, healing crystals, Aunt."

"Elsa-May could use some hearing crystals," Ettie muttered under her breath.

"Wait a minute. They 'think,' or they 'know'?"

Myra continued, "I'm not sure which one. Just let me finish telling you and then you can ask questions. You see, the points of the crystals have power; the energy of the crystal is concentrated on the healing point." She drew a deep breath, and repeated, "The police told me they found poison on the end of a crystal that was with him when he died. That somehow led them to me. Then someone planted that same poison in my home. They must've because I know I never saw that bottle before in my life!"

"How did they get it into your home?" Elsa-May asked.

"And how did they know it was poison without testing it? From what I know, it takes weeks for those kinds of tests to come back," Ettie said.

"I don't know how anyone got in, there was no sign of anything out of place. No sign of a break-in. I don't know the answer to your question, Mother. Perhaps I was in too much shock to hear correctly. My aura was undoubtedly off balance when the police knocked on my door with a search warrant." Myra's lips turned down at the corners. "Will you help me prove my innocence, Ettie?"

Ettie was pleased her daughter came to her every time she had a crisis, but wasn't at all pleased her daughter had chosen to call her 'Ettie,' and sometimes the formal-sounding 'Mother,' instead of the usual *'Mamm,'* which was what everyone in their Amish community called their mothers, and what Myra had grown up calling her. *"Jah,* of course we will."

"Tell us everything from the beginning. Why had this man come to you in the first place?" Elsa-May asked.

"He had a heart problem and had turned away from conventional medicine. Someone told him about me, and I've been treating him for a good year now."

Elsa-May rubbed her chin. "So you said you heal with crystals?"

"Yes, they have healing qualities." She glanced sideways at her mother. "It's an energy thing and I don't expect either of you to understand anything about it."

Elsa-May and Ettie raised their eyebrows at one another.

"What was wrong with the man, was he sick?"

"He had heart problems, Elsa-May. She just said that."

"That's right. He had faith in the crystals, and in my abilities."

Ettie sighed loudly and both Myra and Elsa-May

stared at her. "I'm just sad that you believe all that and didn't follow the way you were raised."

"Let's not get into that now, Mother."

"Now, Myra, I mean, Sparkle, how do you go about healing the man with crystals if he has something wrong with his heart?" Elsa-May took off her glasses, folded them and hooked them over the top of her apron.

"He was a big man, quite overweight and the crystals were restoring balance to his system. He knew he had to lose the weight and no matter how much he dieted, the weight wouldn't budge."

"And who do you think killed him?" Elsa-May asked.

"The wife."

"Why?" Ettie and Elsa-May said at the same time.

"Because, I think she thought that Ian and I were involved. She warned me off him—told me to stay away. I told her there was nothing going on and that I was in a relationship with someone else. She didn't believe me, and it makes sense that she killed him and framed me."

"Who's the detective on the case?" Ettie asked.

"It's the one you know."

"Kelly?" the sisters chimed together, again.

"Yes. That's the one."

"When did this happen?"

"Two days ago. That was when he was murdered, and they found something in my house yesterday. It was a small bottle labeled dimethylmercury. It's a highly toxic heavy metal poison. Just one tiny drop kills on contact."

Ettie said, "Wouldn't Ronald want to know you're in trouble. He could have a word with—."

"I don't want to tell him. He's following some case from years ago that he could never get out of his head. If I tell him, he'll be distracted. I'll handle it alone, with the help of both of you. Anyway, that dimethylmercury they found at my place could've killed me if I'd opened it." Myra trembled. "They have to test it. They seem to think that's what it is. It had a label on it."

"Was someone trying to kill you as well?"

"I don't know, but the police aren't worried about that. They're trying to find my motive for killing Ian." Myra sighed. "I'm a little worried now that the murderer has put that poison on other things around my house. They could've." Myra trembled. "I know I can't worry about that or I'd send myself crazy."

"We'll talk to him and see what we can do," Elsa-May said.

Myra smiled and nodded and then looked at her mother.

"Off course we'll help," Ettie said.

Elsa-May folded her arms over her chest. "Tell me, Sparkle, where would one get one's hands on the poison you mentioned?"

Mrya stared at Elsa-May and blinked a couple of

times. "That's something I don't know. I've been too upset to even think about that."

Ettie stared at her daughter's long pointed-crystal earrings.

Myra frowned at her. "What are you staring at, Mother?"

"Your earrings. Are they real?"

Myra unhooked one earring from her earlobe and held it up in the air. "This is a natural quartz crystal. This is the way it formed in the earth. Stunning, isn't it?"

"It's spectacular," Ettie agreed.

"Some crystals you buy these days have been faceted to look like this, but this one is in its original natural crystal shape."

Ettie put her hand out and Myra placed the crystal in it. Ettie held it up to the light to marvel at God's handiwork. "It's *wunderbaar.*" The crystal was perfectly formed as though it had been fashioned that way. And it had, she thought, by God rather than by man. A loop of silver wound around one end of the crystal, its tail forming a hook for the pierced earlobe.

Myra continued, "And it's special because it's a doubly terminated quartz crystal, meaning it has the pyramid-shaped point at both ends. Same as this one." She touched the other crystal earring that was still in her ear.

"And are they healing?" Elsa-May asked.

Ettie didn't approve of her sister encouraging Myra.

"Oh yes. The energy flows in both directions in a doubly terminated crystal. That's why they're so sought after. You see, the single ones are the more common and are formed against a rock. These ones were formed in a soft substance like clay and that's why they were free to form those shapes on either end."

"How do they form?"

Ettie glared at Elsa-May from behind Myra. Did she have to keep asking questions?

"It happened millions of years ago when the crystals would've been in a molten form and when the mixture cooled down, it formed these shapes. There's a lot more I could tell you, but I doubt you'd find it interesting. Anyway, the crystals increase my psychic abilities by opening my third eye."

Ettie scoffed. "We can't listen to this rubbish."

Myra turned to look at Ettie. "You should open your mind, Mother."

"Not to that nonsense."

Myra tipped her head to one side. "I suppose you don't know what I mean by third eye."

"Enlighten us, Sparkle," Elsa-May said with a grin.

"It's a spiritual eye, not a natural one. It's here." She touched the center of her forehead. "By using my third eye, I can see beyond the earthly dimension into the spiritual world."

"So, you must know who killed him," Elsa-May said.

Ettie cringed when she saw Elsa-May smirking and

that's how she knew her sister only said that to be smart.

Myra nodded, taking what Elsa-May said quite seriously. "I know it's not something you would've heard of before and people are afraid of what they don't know. It's not unusual for them to make jokes about it. Anyway, I do know who did it. It was the wife. Didn't I already say that?"

"*Nee*, you didn't!" Ettie said. "Why do you think she did it?"

"She did, Ettie. She said the wife warned her off him and—"

Ettie nodded. "Now I remember. I'm sorry. I was too busy trying to take everything else in."

"Because you need to clean out your ears, Mother, I'll tell you once more. The wife thought Ian and I were having an affair and she came to warn me off him— told me to stay away. I assured her he was a client and nothing else. I even told her I was seeing Ronald, but she still didn't believe me." Myra sighed.

"That doesn't mean she killed him, though." Ettie handed back the crystal earring.

Myra threaded the silver part of the earring back through the hole in her earlobe. "I know, but I just know Tiffany did it. That's her name, Tiffany Carter. I have a knowledge of it. Tiffany and Ian Carter have a son together named Byron. Ian told me that Tiffany has been worked up about Maria getting her hands on his money. Ian told me that Tiffany keeps asking to see his will and he won't allow her to see it."

"And who's Maria?" Ettie asked.

"She's Ian's first wife. She and Ian have a son together, too, Angelo."

"Let me get this right. Ian was married to a woman called Maria and they had a son, Angelo. Then he was married to wife number two and they also had a son?"

"That's right. One son each."

"Now, the second wife was worried that wife number one wanted to get her hands on the money, so to block her from doing so, she asked to see Ian's will?"

Myra nodded. "That's exactly right."

"How long has Ian been seeking treatment with you?" Ettie asked.

"About a year and he swore he felt better. Well, he did, until he was murdered. He came twice a week for two hours at a time. He was always the last appointment of the day and once it was over we'd sip green tea and share snippets of our lives in the sunroom."

"And he had a lot of money?" Elsa-May asked. "What Ettie and I have found out by experience is this; when someone is murdered, it's mostly over love, or money."

"Sometimes revenge," Ettie added. "Or any combination of those three."

"Yes, Aunt, he had enough money for someone to kill him over."

"What did he do for a living to get so much money?" Ettie asked.

"He owned an engineering firm and then he sold it."

"To whom did he leave his money?" Elsa-May asked.

"My psychic abilities tell me he left most of it to Tiffany and their son."

"What about the other wife and son? Maria, and was it Angelo?"

"That's right, Mother." Myra shook her head. "I don't know how you can remember something about complete strangers and don't remember anything about me."

Ettie pursed her lips not knowing what she was talking about and not game to ask. "I'll try to remember your new name. Sparkle Orient. You'll have that one for a while, will you?"

"Yes, Mother. I've got no intention of changing it. After all, I chose it myself. I'm sure Maria and Angelo would've been left something."

"Ettie and I will visit Detective Kelly and see what we can find out."

"Did Kelly remember you?" Ettie asked Myra.

"He thought he knew me from somewhere. I had to tell him who I was and then he remembered."

Elsa-May nodded. "He should be expecting us then."

"Would you like a cup of tea, Myra ... I mean ... um ..."

Myra rolled her eyes. "Sparkle, Mother, it's Sparkle, and I'd like a green tea if you have it."

"We don't," Elsa-May said. "We can give you black tea, or *kaffe,* or a glass of milk."

"Dairy? Don't tell me you eat dairy."

"Jah, we do."

Myra shook her head. "You should be aware of the latest research."

"We'll read the latest research as soon as we start wearing crystals and locate all three eyes," Elsa-May said.

At that, Ettie jumped to her feet. "How about a weak black tea, Sparkle?"

"That'll be fine, thanks."

Ettie hurried to the kitchen, glad that Myra—Ettie decided her daughter would always be Myra—hadn't reacted badly to what Elsa-May had just said. As she put the teakettle on the stove, she wondered how she could have produced a child so different from herself. What attracted Myra to the rubbish she was now talking about? That was a big question, one to ponder at another time. For now, they had to get Myra out of trouble. If only Detective Kelly wasn't the lead detective on the case. Why couldn't it have been someone else?

CHAPTER 2

ETTIE TOOK a tray of tea out to the living room and placed it on a low table.

"Thank you, Mother." Myra picked up the cup of tea and took a sip. "Not bad."

Ettie gave Elsa-May a cup of tea and sat down with one for herself. "Like Elsa-May said, we'll pay Detective Kelly a visit tomorrow to find out what's happening."

"Tomorrow? Oh, thank you." Myra took another sip of tea. "Don't you have any cookies?"

"We do, but I didn't think you'd want to eat them."

"I do. I would like one to eat with my tea. I always like to have a little something with my tea."

"Coming up," Ettie said.

"Stay there, Ettie, I'll get it." Elsa-May pushed herself up out of her chair.

Ettie was a little apprehensive to be left there with

Myra. "Don't worry, Sparkle. I'm certain everything will be okay."

"Easy for you to say. You're not the one they think has murdered someone."

Ettie shook her head. "It's not easy seeing one of your children in trouble."

"That's something I'll never know because I'm too old to be a mother now. Thanks for reminding me."

Ettie leaned back on the couch and stared at her teacup. Sometimes it was easier not to say anything at all.

"Here you are," Elsa-May breezed into the room with a plate of sugar cookies and chocolate chip cookies. "Your mother and I just made these yesterday."

"They do look delicious. I'll have to have one of each," Myra said with a girlish giggle.

Ettie wasn't brave enough to comment about the weight Myra had lost, and wondered if she might have been on some special diet.

"Is there anything else you can tell us about Ian?" Elsa-May asked as she sat back down.

"He was approaching his fifty-second birthday. He has one son with Maria and one son with his current wife, but I've already told you that much. I know a lot about him. It just depends on what's relevant."

"Are you still living in the same place?" Ettie asked.

"I'll write down the address for you if you give me a bit of paper."

Ettie placed her teacup down and shuffled over to

the bureau to find pen and paper and then took them back and placed them on the low table in front of Myra.

"What does his current wife do?" Elsa-May asked.

"Apart from being a socialite and attending all the parties and charity events, she owns a small but very upmarket clothing boutique in the Winston Hotel. Ian didn't go out so much. In fact, he hated attending those functions."

"Does that mean husband and wife didn't get along?" Elsa-May asked.

"He never said too much, just enough so I got the idea there was tension there."

"What gave you that idea?" Ettie asked.

"He told me what I just told you about the will, and I know that they lived at opposite ends of their mansion. He had his wing, and she had another."

"So, you think she was in the marriage for the money?"

"I know it," Myra said just before she placed half a cookie into her mouth. "Mmm, these are delicious," she mumbled around the bite of cookie.

"Why don't we visit you after we talk to the detective tomorrow?"

Myra swallowed her mouthful of cookie and had another sip of tea. "Good idea." That prompted Myra to write down her address. "I'm not too far away," she said as she wrote. She set the pen back on the table and passed the slip of paper back to Ettie.

Ettie looked at the address, a little sad that she hardly ever saw Myra even though they lived close. "We'll visit you late tomorrow afternoon and let you know what he says."

"On second thought, I have a busy day tomorrow. I won't even get a lunch break. I've got appointments nine through five." Myra sighed. "That is, if my day isn't disrupted by being arrested."

"Why don't you stop by for dinner tomorrow night? You can have the evening meal here and, hopefully, we would know something from Detective Kelly by then," Elsa-May said.

Myra gave a weak smile. "Thanks, Aunt, I'll do that. I should go."

The elderly sisters followed Myra to the door. They stood together and watched Myra speed away in her vibrant red sports car.

"Well, well. Sparkle Orient." Elsa-May stared after the car.

"Jah, I don't know what to say about that. Do you think she just wants to shock me, or wants to hurt me?"

"Do you want to know the truth?"

Ettie faced her sister. "What is it?"

"I think she gives very little thought to you at all. Except when she's in trouble."

It was true. Ettie knew that what Elsa-May said was a fact.

"We have to figure out what we're having for dinner tomorrow night. Any ideas?"

"What did we have planned?"

"Meatloaf. The meatloaf I made today will be enough for tomorrow and if we're going out, we'll have no time to cook."

Ettie nodded. "Then we should stick with that, but nothing with dairy in it for dessert. Apparently, she doesn't drink milk any longer."

Elsa-May chuckled as she closed the front door. "Sit down, Ettie, and I'll make you a cup of nice hot tea."

"We've only just had one."

"I'm having another. We need it after hearing all that."

"Denke, that'd be nice. I suppose we'll have to take the pie for the neighbors later."

"We?" Elsa-May asked.

"You." Ettie chuckled.

Elsa-May continued into the kitchen while Ettie patted Snowy who was still on the couch after being patted by Myra. "You're such a spoiled dog, Snowy."

Snowy remained silent with his eyes closed. His cute little tail gave one little wag.

THE NEXT DAY, Ettie and Elsa-May sat opposite Detective Kelly with his desk separating him from them. Ettie was a little annoyed because they had waited for over an hour to see him.

"I already know why you two are here."

"That's right. It's about Myra," Elsa-May said.

Ettie stared at her sister. "Don't you mean Sparkle?"

"Sparkle Orient," Detective Kelly stated.

"That's right," Elsa-May said.

He stared at Ettie. "That's your daughter, Ettie."

"I know." Ettie bit her lip. "But sometimes I do wonder ..."

The detective continued, "Allegations have been made."

Elsa-May leaned forward. "What allegations and who has made them?"

Ettie's heart thumped hard. Myra hadn't mentioned anything about allegations.

"Ian Carter confessed to his wife that he and Sparkle were plotting to murder her with a dangerous chemical and she gave us the name of it. The plan was, Ian was supposed to lure Sandra—"

"Sandra?" Elsa-May interrupted.

Kelly frowned and sifted through his paperwork. "Ah, sorry. Mrs. Carter's name is Tiffany. I'm not sure where I got the name Sandra. Anyway, according to Mrs. Carter, Ian confessed that Sparkle and he had planned that he would encourage Tiffany to have an appointment with Sparkle where she would do a treatment on her. She'd then give her a poison-tipped crystal to take home with her to continue the treatment. According to Tiffany, Ian confessed that Sparkle and he were going to kill her."

Elsa-May scoffed. "Sounds a bit hit and miss for a murder plot, don't you think so, Detective?"

"No comment. That's the allegation. We—"

"If Ian wanted his wife killed why couldn't he have put that poison on her himself? Why did he need Myra? Um, Sparkle?" Elsa-May asked. "And why would he tell her that even if he changed his mind? Why not just keep silent?"

Kelly frowned at her. "That's what she told us. We did find something suspicious at Sparkle's residence, and I suppose she has told you that we took the bottle away for testing."

"Let's wind back a minute. What happened after Ian told his wife this? What did she do with that information?" Elsa-May asked.

Ettie put her hand on Elsa-May's arm to calm her down.

Kelly frowned. "Nothing. He confessed his plot, apologized, and then they reconciled. They were going through a rocky period a few months back, she told me."

Ettie shook her head. "If my husband had confessed that he and another woman were going to kill me, there would be no going back from that. I'd move out of the house immediately."

Detective Kelly raised his eyebrows. "I thought that wouldn't be allowed for you in your—"

"We can't divorce. We can separate and never marry again."

Elsa-May added, "Unless the spouse dies, in which case the other party is free to remarry."

"Ah, I see. Yes, I would be the same, Mrs. Smith. I don't think I would ever trust my wife again if she confessed such a thing to me."

"Yes. It's quite unbelievable," Elsa-May added.

"And doesn't it usually take weeks for toxicology reports to come back?" Ettie asked.

"Sometimes. We're still waiting on confirmation, but we're going on what Mrs. Carter has said. Sparkle had the bottle in her house with a label on it and it was the same poison that Mrs. Carter told us that her husband mentioned they were plotting to kill her with."

"She was the one who named that poison?" Ettie asked.

"That's right."

"Phooey!" Elsa-May blurted out. "She's making it all up."

"Of course she'd be making it up," Ettie agreed. "My daughter is no killer. That poison was obviously planted there to make her look guilty." Ettie looked nervously at Detective Kelly, hoping he would agree.

He leaned back in his chair. "It might surprise you, Mrs. Smith. People constantly surprise me. My belief now is that anyone can kill under the right circumstances."

Ettie was worried that they weren't being much help to Myra.

"Sparkle was at our place yesterday, and she told us there was some conflict between the first wife and the second wife," Elsa-May said.

He nodded, leaned forward again and placed his hands on the desk. "We're looking into every possibility. Now, if you ladies will excuse me, I've got a job to do." When neither made a move to leave, he added, "I've got a lot of work to do. Will you please let me do my job?"

"Yes, of course," Ettie said.

"Will you keep us updated, please?" Elsa-May asked.

"I will, through Sparkle," he said with a weak smile.

Ettie bounded to her feet, and she and Elsa-May headed out of the station.

CHAPTER 3

As THEY WERE WALKING down the steps outside the station, Ettie asked, "What do you think, Elsa-May?"

"Why would the man have told his own wife that he and Myra were plotting to kill her? I just can't say 'Sparkle' again right now."

"Tiffany was obviously lying, and I hope Kelly realizes that. And I've heard enough 'Sparkle' for now, too."

"Well, but what if she wasn't lying? What if her husband actually told her that?" Elsa-May asked.

Ettie thought for a moment as they walked up the road together. "For attention?"

"Maybe to jolt her into paying him more attention, which is a bad way to go about things, for sure and for certain. I can't think of another reason, though."

Ettie tapped a finger on her chin. "Let's see; he confessed to her that he and Myra had planned to lure her into Myra's place of work where she'd be given a treatment and then she'd be sent away with a poisoned crystal? Why would someone tell someone that?"

"To make her jealous of Myra?"

"That's right, Elsa-May. That's what I thought."

"So, either Mr. Carter was lying or Mrs. Carter was lying. And the only reason we can come up with Mr. Carter lying is that he was doing it for attention, aside from the stupidity of the idea, and if Mrs. Carter was lying she's trying to implicate Myra in the murder ... right?" Elsa-May asked.

Ettie nodded. "I think so, but she could have been fixated on him spending so much time at Sparkle's place, so that could be a reason why he might have come up with that idea. I can't believe I just called Myra by that silly name."

"Never mind the name for now. And if he didn't say it, Mrs. Carter was making the whole thing up, which means she's guilty of his murder."

"Maybe she's not guilty," Ettie said.

"*Jah,* maybe she just made the whole thing up because she was annoyed with Myra, or didn't like her, and she wants Myra to get the blame for his murder."

Ettie stared at Elsa-May, "What did you just say?"

Elsa-May huffed. "I don't know why I bother talking if you're not listening."

"I am—I was. I got distracted for a moment thinking about whether we should go home or go to the coffee shop up the road."

"That's an easy decision! Go to the coffee shop up

the road, of course. And I can repeat what I said to you while we're walking there."

"We'll share a cake," Ettie said, worried about her sister's increasing girth.

"We'll have one each and share as usual."

Ettie grimaced. "I think we should just have one."

Elsa-May looked sad.

"You can choose," Ettie said, which made Elsa-May smile again. "Now, what did you say?"

"I forget myself." Elsa-May adjusted her prayer *kapp*. "Let's see now … that's right; I said, what if she didn't like Myra and just wants her to get the blame for the murder?"

"That would mean Mrs. Carter would be letting the real murderer go free. I'm sorry, but that just doesn't make sense." Ettie shook her head. "She's guilty. There's no other option because we know Myra didn't do it."

"Hmm. What if she knows the person and doesn't want them to get into trouble?"

Ettie's eyebrows rose, nearly touching the edge of her prayer *kapp*. "To protect her son, Byron?"

"Quite possibly," Elsa-May said.

"That all fits in. Either she is the guilty one, or she's protecting her son."

"Great, I'll tell Kelly we've solved his case for him, shall I?" Elsa-May said sarcastically. She smiled to make it clear that she was teasing.

Ettie giggled. "Not before cake."

"Quite right. Cake always comes first because we

have to eat. And then what do you say about paying a little visit to Mrs. Carter?"

"What?" Ettie hoped Elsa-May wasn't serious.

"We can't sit back and do nothing. We have to try something. Or do you want Sparkle to rot in jail for a crime—"

"Okay. I'll do it," Ettie agreed. "As soon as we finish this, we'll find her address from the telephone book in the library or from their computer."

"Good." Elsa-May pushed the door of the café open. They stood in front of the glass cake-display cabinet for a while before they placed their order. Elsa-May conceded and decided to go along with Ettie's idea of only having one slice of cake and sharing it. Elsa-May's final choice, with Ettie's full approval, was an orange poppy seed cake with thick cream-cheese frosting, and they ordered hot tea for two.

They chose a table by the window.

Ettie retied the strings of her *kapp* so they wouldn't dangle in the tea when it came. "I'm a bit worried about talking with Mrs. Carter. What should we say?"

"I don't know. Something will come to us at the time. Anyway, she might not be home."

When their order came, Elsa-May took a knife and cut the cake directly down the center. She took a slice for herself and put Ettie's on a separate plate.

"You haven't taken the biggest half, have you?"

Elsa-May pressed her lips together and swapped slices.

"I'm only joking." Ettie was surprised her sister was in such a serious mood.

"It's hard to know with you sometimes." Elsa-May stuck her fork into the cake. "So, back to Mrs. Carter. What do we say?"

"You got the idea to go there, so it's only fair that you come up with what to say." Ettie sipped her tea.

"I would just go knock on her door." Elsa-May asked.

"And then?"

"We should start the conversation by saying we're collecting for charity."

Ettie didn't want to tell a lie. "And would that be true?"

"If she gives us any money I'm sure we can find a charitable cause to pass it along to."

"You're right, like the volunteer firefighters."

"Exactly," Elsa-May pushed a large portion of cake into her mouth.

Ettie put both elbows on the table. "And then how do we go from asking Mrs. Carter for a donation to asking her if she killed her husband?"

While she chewed, Elsa-May stared at Ettie. After she swallowed, she answered, "I don't know."

Ettie sighed. "Then there's no point seeing her, is there?"

"*Jah* there is. We'll have to think of something. She might even ask us into the house while she goes to fetch her money."

"You're having delusions if you think Mrs. Carter is going to invite us into her home. A couple of old ladies she doesn't even know. Old age is finally—"

"We have to do something—try something."

Ettie sighed. "I just would like more to go on. It would be nice if we knew someone who knew her."

"Well, we don't! We either go there and knock on her door or sit here on our backsides and do nothing. We might find a clue if we go to the house, that's all I'm saying." Elsa-May pushed the last mouthful of cake into her mouth.

"Okay."

Elsa-May set her beady blue eyes onto her sister. "Okay?"

"We'll say we're there for donations." Ettie gave a huge sigh. Elsa-May was right. As much as she hated the idea of turning up on Tiffany Carter's doorstep, they had to do something.

CHAPTER 4

LATER THAT AFTERNOON, Ettie and Elsa-May were standing outside Mrs. Carter's house after finding the address by using one of the public library computers.

"I hope she's wasting time. I mean, I hope we're not wasting our time."

"We'll soon find out." Elsa-May pushed Ettie forward.

"Why do I have to go first? You're the older *schweschder.*"

"That's right, and as the elder I'm telling you to go first."

Ettie adjusted her prayer *kapp,* smoothed down her apron and walked toward the door, dragging her feet. Her head swam thinking of things she could say. Then a thought occurred to her. If Mrs. Carter opened the door and she didn't speak, Elsa-May would have to say something. Ettie reached the large wood panelled door and knocked twice, loud enough to be heard from the other end of the house.

"That's not loud enough, Ettie. You want her to hear it, don't you? Knock like you mean it." Elsa-May pushed her out of the way and knocked more loudly.

"She's not home."

The sisters jumped, and looked to their right from where the sudden voice had come. It was a hunched over lady of approximately seventy years, wearing a long gray cardigan and a striped multi-colored knitted hat. The hat reminded Ettie of Joseph's coat of many colors.

"That's a shame," Elsa-May said as she stepped toward the lady. "Do you know when they'll be back?"

Ettie said, "We want to talk to Mr. Carter. Do you know when he'll be home?"

"He's dead," she said.

"Really?" Ettie tried to look surprised and hoped this woman could tell them something. She looked like the kind of woman who meddled in her neighbors' lives.

"Oh dear," Elsa-May said with her hand to her cheek.

The woman nodded. "It's true."

"That must've been sudden," Ettie said.

"Do you know Mrs. Carter?"

"Only Mr. Carter," Ettie said.

The neighbor took another step toward them. "She killed him, she did."

"Who did?" Elsa-May asked.

The old lady looked around carefully and then walked all the way to the fence. "Tiffany Carter killed him. It wasn't a love match. I used to work for them until they got rid of me. Now I work here." She tossed her head to one side toward the next-door house. "I'm a housekeeper. Have been for about fifty years."

"You used to work for the Carters?" Elsa-May asked.

"Yep. Until she got rid of me. I heard her plotting to kill him around five years ago with someone called Harrison."

"Did you call the police?"

"I did, and she told them I had dementia, and then later, she got rid of me." She narrowed her eyes at them. "What did you want with Mr. Carter?"

"We wondered if he would make a donation to the volunteer firefighters organization."

"Not likely, now that he's dead. And she wouldn't give you the smell of her supper."

"Thank you, Mrs. ..."

"Alice."

"Thank you, Alice," Elsa-May said.

"Have the police questioned you since Mr. Carter's death, Alice?" Ettie asked.

"Nope."

Ettie stepped forward and placed her hands on top of the four-foot-high fence. "Alice, the truth of the matter is that we really aren't here asking for donations."

Her mouth tightened and she gave Elsa-May a quick glance before she looked back at Ettie. "You're not?"

"No, we're not and we know Mr. Carter has died because the police think my daughter had something to do with his death. Mrs. Carter told them things to make my daughter look guilty."

"Would you tell the police what you know?" Elsa-May asked. "It would really help my niece."

"Sure will. If you think they'll listen. Only thing is, I don't want my employers to think I'm a tattler."

"When do you finish work today?"

"I live here and never go anywhere. I work all the time."

"Surely you get a break. What if my sister and I take you out tomorrow?"

"Where?"

"The police station and then we'll take you to a delightful cake shop."

"The best cake shop," Elsa-May added.

"Mrs. Marlborough plays bridge Thursday afternoons and she doesn't need me then."

"It's Thursday tomorrow," Elsa-May said.

"Who should I speak with when I get there?"

"Detective Kelly is handling the case."

Alice nodded. "Kelly. Okay. Tell him I'll be there at two."

"Shall we collect you and take you in?"

A smile softened her face. "If it's not too much trouble, that would be splendid."

Ettie said, "It's no trouble. We'll see you tomorrow just before two."

"And leave enough room for cake," Elsa-May said which made Alice's face light up.

Alice turned away and started sweeping the path and Ettie and Elsa-May left the Carters' property.

"See, Ettie? I told you that things would be good if we went there."

"*Jah*, it was a good idea. *Denke,* Elsa-May. You're so much braver than I."

"Now we have to make sure Kelly will be at the station at two."

"He will be if we tell him Alice is coming, and that she made a report about what she heard five years ago. I'm surprised he didn't know that. He should've had a record of that complaint being made."

"He probably does, Ettie, but just didn't mention it to us. He could have her on his list to interview for all we know. I hope he's not going to be mad at us."

WHEN THEY FOUND A PUBLIC PHONE, they called for a taxi. While waiting for it they called Detective Kelly. Detective Kelly didn't seem very impressed to hear something from a former housekeeper, but nevertheless, he agreed to talk with Alice the next day.

Ettie hung up the phone. "That didn't go very well."

"Don't be troubled. Nothing ever goes well with him."

"Let's collect a few things from the markets."

"Good idea. I feel like a boiled fruit cake," Elsa-May said.

"And we need green tea for Myra."

THEY ARRIVED home to see their front door open. They hurried through their garden gate and when they reached the stairs of their porch they smelled smoke.

CHAPTER 5

"Do you smell that?" Elsa-May asked Ettie.

"I do." Ettie stared at the open front door. There was definitely smoke coming from somewhere.

The sisters hurried into the house, fearing it was on fire.

What they saw was Myra holding something in her left hand, an object that was putting out smoke. She fanned the smoke everywhere around her with the other hand.

When Ettie got closer, she saw Myra was waving a large mottled-gray feather to disperse the smoke. "What's going on?" Ettie placed the shopping bags on the floor. "What's all this smoke?"

"I'm saging the house to clear the negative energy build-up. Your house probably needs more than a sage clearing because it's got years of built up—"

"We don't want that smelly stuff in our house," Elsa-May spat out.

Myra frowned. "There's nothing wrong with it. It's clearing the energy."

"We like the energy just how it is and you're scaring Snowy." Elsa-May pointed to her dog that was cowering in the corner with his tail between his legs.

Myra shook her head. "Okay. It's your choice. I'm just trying to make the place more comfortable for you, and for me while I'm here."

"Thanks for your thoughts," Ettie said. "I'll get the dinner on. Is reheated meatloaf okay?"

"Sounds delicious, Mother."

Elsa-May talked to Myra in the living room while Ettie unpacked the shopping, reheated the meatloaf and prepared the accompanying vegetables. When everything was almost ready, Elsa-May and Myra came into the kitchen and sat down at the table.

"Sparkle wants to know what we learned today, Ettie."

Ettie sat down with them while the vegetables finished cooking. "We came across a neighbor who used to work for the Carters. She believes that Mrs. Carter killed him, just like you do."

Myra folded her arms. "That's nice to know. Does she have any kind of proof?"

Ettie and Elsa-May glanced at one another. There was no proof, only the word of an old lady and they knew what Detective Kelly thought about old ladies.

"No, but—"

Myra narrowed her eyes. "It's just her say-so then?"

Elsa-May fixed a bright smile on her face. "That's it, but it's got to help. She's seeing Kelly tomorrow at two."

"I appreciate you both trying to help. Truly I do, but I don't see that what she's going to say will make any difference at all." Myra threw her hands in the air and lowered them back to the table.

Elsa-May reached over and patted her hand. "Why don't we wait and see?"

Myra offered her aunt a weak smile and nodded. "I hope something comes of it, but luck's just not on my side at the moment. I don't have much faith."

"All you need is the faith the size of a mustard seed," Elsa-May said.

"Thanks, I know you're trying to be helpful, but I just don't connect with all that anymore."

"Maybe all this happened as a sign."

"A sign?"

"A sign that maybe you should try putting your trust in Him once more."

Myra didn't answer; instead she sat there nibbling nervously on a fingernail.

THE NEXT DAY, Ettie and Elsa-May collected Alice in a taxi, and drove to the police station. Once the taxi stopped in front of the station, Alice leaped out of the car and headed up the steps of the station before them. Ettie settled-up with the driver and then the sisters followed her.

Alice spoke to the officer at the desk and he pointed to the waiting area.

The sisters walked across and sat either side of Alice.

"Did you ask for Detective Kelly and say you had an appointment?"

Alice nodded. "Yes. I've been giving things a lot of thought and I'm certain it was the son."

"What was?" Ettie asked.

"The person who killed Ian was the son."

"Yesterday you said the wife," Ettie whispered.

"And someone called Harrison," Elsa-May added.

"That was before I remembered something about the son."

"Which one?" Elsa-May asked.

"Did I tell you that Mr. Carter said he was leaving me a little something in his will? I'm excited to see what it is."

Right at that moment, Detective Kelly appeared and Alice was ushered into his office.

"Which son?" Elsa-May stared at Ettie.

"I don't know. Why did she change her mind? Yesterday she said it was the wife."

Elsa-May made tsk tsk sounds. "This isn't good. Now Kelly won't believe her since she's flip-flopped.

We told him she thought it was the wife who killed him."

"Don't panic yet. We'll feed her cake and find out exactly what she said to Kelly."

Ettie and Elsa-May stayed in their chairs, staring at the corridor and waiting for Alice to come out.

"We should've found out more about the sons," Elsa-May said.

"I know, but Alice should know a lot about both sons and both of the wives if she was the housekeeper there for years. She strikes me as the kind of person who notices everything."

Half an hour later, Alice came out of the office by herself and walked back into the waiting area. Kelly didn't even follow her to talk with them.

"It's all over," Alice said.

"What is?"

"My interview. He said it's all over and that I could go."

"Okay. Let's go have coffee," Elsa-May said, pushing herself to her feet

Alice smiled. "That sounds like a good idea to me. Wait!"

The sisters stared at Alice.

"He wants to speak to both of you." She sat down. "I'll wait right here until you're finished. I don't want to miss out on the cake. I told him you were both waiting here and you'd brought me here in a taxi and he said to tell you he's in his office."

Reluctantly, both sisters walked into Kelly's office and saw him standing there with hands-on hips and his cheeks bright red. Ettie knew that wasn't good. Every time he got angry, his face got beet red. They both cowered in the doorway.

He pointed to the chairs on the other side of his desk. "SIT!"

They wasted no time doing what they were told.

He paced up and down for a few moments before he sat on the edge of his chair. "Why would you waste my time by bringing that old gossip in to talk to me?"

Elsa-May said, "She's not an old gossip. She worked for Ian Carter's family for years. She watched Ian grow up. And then she worked for him."

Ettie added, "She said that Ian was going to leave her a little something in the will."

Kelly scoffed. "A little something is right."

"She has been left something?" Ettie asked.

"I can't tell you that, Mrs. Smith. What I can tell you is that what she told me was nothing like what you claimed yesterday that she told you."

Ettie looked away from the detective, disappointed that Alice had let them down by changing her story.

"And then do you know what she told me?"

After a long silence, Elsa-May asked, "What?"

"She told me she only came to talk with me because both of you had promised her cake and coffee up the road. What do you think about that?"

Elsa-May grimaced. "It wasn't a bribe, or anything."

He glowered. "It certainly sounds like a bribe to me."

"It wasn't," Ettie said quietly.

"We only brought her here because of what she told us."

"If you want to help, stay out of my way, so I can investigate this. All right?" When no one said anything, the detective repeated. "All right, Mrs. Smith?"

Ettie nodded and looked away from him.

"Mrs. Lutz?"

Elsa-May nodded as well.

"Come on, Elsa-May. Let's go."

"Yes, you've got to pay out on that bribe waiting at the coffee shop, no doubt." Kelly pressed his thin lips together.

"Have you tried their orange cake?" Elsa-May smiled at Kelly.

Ettie tugged on her sleeve. She couldn't believe her sister. Nothing they said would make him happy at this time. The only thing they could do to improve matters was leave. Besides, the detective had no time to be chatting about cake while a murderer was on the loose. As soon as they found the real killer, Myra would be off the hook. "Not the right time." Ettie walked out of Kelly's office closely followed by Elsa-May.

"I don't know if I've ever seen him that cross," Elsa-May said as they walked back to the waiting area.

"Me either. Now where has Alice gotten herself to?"

They looked all around the waiting area and then walked to the exit.

Elsa-May dug Ettie in the ribs.

"Ow! What did you do that for?"

"Because I see her. There she is, over there." Ettie pointed to Alice waiting on a seat outside the police station. When she saw them, she gave them a little wave and walked over.

"Now where is this cake shop you've been telling me about?"

CHAPTER 6

ONCE THEY WERE SEATED with cake and coffee, Elsa-May launched into her questions. "Alice, what makes you think that one of Ian's sons killed him?"

"For the money. You see, the son by the first wife was not bothered by money. He's a free spirit and probably lives in a tent somewhere with his long hair, his crystals and banging on his tribal drum."

"Drum?"

"Crystals?" Ettie asked.

"Yes. He belonged to some kind of society where they use crystals and they chant, or something along those lines."

"Meditate?" Elsa-May asked.

"That too, most likely. It was his son from his second marriage who was the greedy one. You mark my words." Alice wagged a finger at them.

Ettie tried hard to think of the son's name but couldn't remember it. She remembered that the son from the first marriage was Angelo. "Did you overhear anything that was said, such as a plot to murder Ian?"

"I hear a lot of things. Housekeepers always do." She cut a large bite of cake and popped it into her mouth.

Elsa-May took a turn in asking the questions. "Yesterday you were convinced that the wife murdered him. What made you change your mind?"

She held a hand up to stop Elsa-May from talking while she proceeded to savor the mouthful. When she had swallowed, she patted around the edges of her mouth with a paper napkin before she spoke. "I overheard Ian—Mr. Carter— saying he wanted to leave me a little something. This was years ago when he was updating his will. Tiffany was horrified and got all hot under the collar and somehow managed to talk him out of it."

"And?" Elsa-May asked.

"And then, they got rid of me—Mrs. Carter did."

Ettie leaned forward. "What did Mr. Carter have to say about you leaving?"

"He was upset, but right after the will incident, Mrs. Carter concocted a story about me stealing." Alice shook her head in disgust. "He didn't believe it, thankfully, but to keep the peace and to keep Tiffany happy, he had to let me go. He convinced the Marlboroughs next door to take me on as their housekeeper. Ian told me on the quiet he'd still leave me a little something in his will and Tiffany never need learn of it, and he also said if I ever needed anything to come to him. He knew he'd most likely die before me because of his heart."

"That was decent of him," Ettie said.

Elsa-May pursed her lips. "Yes, she never would learn of it until he died."

Alice nodded.

"How much longer will you work?" Elsa-May asked. "Do you intend to retire?"

"I'll have to at some point. I'll work as long as I can. If I didn't work, I'd have nothing to do. I'd like to travel but don't have the money. I have no family, so I'd have nothing to fill my days with. I like to be useful. I worked for Ian's parents right up until they died. I've watched him grow from a boy into a man."

"Can I ask what you said to the detective about Byron killing his father?"

"I simply told Detective Kelly how Byron's mother lied and that he was after his father's money and didn't want anyone else to have a share."

Ettie was deeply disappointed. There was no proof or anything. No wonder Kelly was so upset. "Can we keep in contact with you, Alice?"

"Of course, you can. I'll write down the number of my cell phone. I'm sure you don't want your daughter to be accused of anything. If I can help, I'll do anything I can."

"Thank you. That's good of you." Ettie wrote down

their address for Alice, explaining that they had no phone.

"Maybe we can have afternoon tea again some time."

Elsa-May nodded. "That would be nice."

"I'll find my own way home. There are a few things I want to pick up from the stores. Thanks for a lovely outing."

WHEN ALICE GOT INTO A BUS, the two sisters walked up the road. "Elsa-May, after listening to what Alice had to say, I think we should stop by the station and apologize to Detective Kelly for wasting his time. We need to keep on his good side."

Elsa-May shuddered. "You can. I'll wait outside."

"*Nee,* I'm not going unless you come with me. Think of it this way, when Myra comes to our house tonight with her pointed crystals and her billowing smoke, what are we going to tell her?"

"It's Sparkle."

Ettie rolled her eyes.

"Hmm. You're right. She'll think we've made things worse for her."

"Exactly. Now, pull yourself together and follow me." Ettie marched ahead and Elsa-May walked quickly behind her.

When they got back to the police station, they were informed Kelly had left the building. The sisters chose to wait for him to return even though the officer on the desk had no idea when that would be.

"Just as well we've had some substance," Elsa-May said as she once again sat on one of the hard-plastic seats in the waiting area.

"Don't you mean sustenance?"

Elsa-May giggled. "What did I say?"

"Substance."

"Well, I suppose that's correct as well. We had food and that was our substance and our sustenance." She giggled. "The substance of our sustenance."

Ettie blew out a deep breath. Elsa-May could turn anything around to suit herself. She never liked to be wrong about anything. Elsa-May then handed Ettie a handkerchief.

Ettie took it and held it in the air. "What's this for?"

"You've got crumbs around your mouth."

"You're only telling me this now?" Ettie dabbed at her mouth with the corners of the handkerchief.

"I didn't notice before."

Ettie finished wiping her face and tucked the handkerchief inside her sleeve. "Better?" She turned to face her sister, who proceeded to straighten Ettie's prayer *kapp.* Ettie slapped her hands away. "I meant are there any more crumbs."

"Nee." Elsa-May's eyes dropped to her shoulders. "Only on the top of your cape." She raised a hand to wipe them off.

"Don't," Ettie whispered looking down at her shoulders. "There's nothing there."

"I can see them."

"Well, if I can't I'm not going to worry about them."

"As you wish. I'm just trying to help."

Ettie sighed and shifted in her seat wondering how Elsa-May could see such small things without the help of her glasses. "These seats are so hard." It was all right for Elsa-May who had enough of her own padding, but the chairs were starting to give Ettie a sore behind. "I hope we don't have to wait too long."

"He always comes back to the office, doesn't he, before he goes home?"

Ettie nodded. "I think so. He's always complaining that he's got so much paperwork. I think that's the last thing he does before he goes home. And now he's going home to that new wife of his."

"Hmm. I wonder how that's working out. They hardly knew one another before they got married."

"People within our community marry without getting to know one another very well."

Elsa-May swiped a hand through the air. "That's different. We have the same basic beliefs and live by the same principles as the people we marry."

"I suppose that's true, so no one is really a stranger. Isn't it awful how Mrs. Carter said that Alice stole something?"

"It's unfair, but we're talking about the same woman who also told outrageous lies about Sparkle. It is sad that poor old Alice lost her job with the Carter family since she'd been working for them for so long," Elsa-May said.

"It's convenient for us, though, that she stayed close."

"Close enough to keep up with the gossip about the family?"

Ettie nodded. *"Jah."*

Elsa-May clasped her hands together. "I don't know if we can go by anything she says since she changes her stories all the time. It makes me think that that's all they are, just stories." With a loud sigh, she then said, "I wish I had brought my knitting. I'm not used to sitting around doing nothing when I could be doing something."

"You're always knitting and complaining of sore fingers. This will give your fingers a rest."

"I suppose so, but it might be good exercise for them. I'm thinking of making teddy bears for the Children's Hospital like Michelle suggested."

Ettie wasn't really listening. She was too busy staring at all the people who came into the station, wondering why they would say a few words to the sergeant on the desk and then leave. Then when she felt Elsa-May staring at her, she realized her sister was waiting for her to comment. "The Children's Hospital did you say?"

"Michelle is organizing it."

"That figures. Michelle is always organizing something. She probably organizes her twelve children's visits to the bathroom each day. Come to think of it, where does she find the time to do anything outside the *haus* with all those *kinner,* and her in-laws living with them?"

"It sounds like you're jealous, Ettie."

Ettie frowned at her sister, who was grinning at her. *"Jah,* I'm jealous."

When Elsa-May chuckled, Ettie grew irritated because she'd said it sarcastically, but Elsa-May probably thought she was actually jealous. She couldn't let the moment pass without setting her sister straight. "Why would I be jealous about someone organizing a bunch of old ladies to make teddy bears? Anyway, what does the bishop say about teddy bears? I don't think it's appropriate." Ettie pursed her lips and looked straight ahead.

"He says nothing. They're for the hospital—for the children."

"Jah. I understood that the first time you said it. Making teddy bears for the children who are in the Children's Hospital—got it."

"Why do you begrudge the children having a little happiness? It's something I can do that is useful, bringing a smile to a sick child's face—"

"Hush, Elsa-May, enough. You're always doing this."

"What? Doing what? I haven't started making the teddy bears yet."

"This is what you're like when you have nothing to

do. You start picking over nothing at all. I'm not going to sit around and listen to this nonsense." Ettie bounded to her feet, took two steps and then the detective walked in the door and locked eyes with her. She quickly wiped off the grim expression on her face and replaced it with a bright smile. "Good morning, Detective."

CHAPTER 7

Kelly frowned at Ettie with a raised eyebrow, glanced at Elsa-May behind her, and finally said, "Afternoon, Mrs. Smith."

"Oh yes. It would be afternoon by now, wouldn't it? Good afternoon." Out of the corner of Ettie's eye, she saw Elsa-May push herself up off her chair. Ettie thought she better say why they were there before Elsa-May put her foot in it again. "Can we have a quick word with you, Detective?"

"It better be quick. In my office?"

"Yes." Ettie nodded. They followed Detective Kelly through to his office and he closed the door. Ettie sat down first.

Kelly stared at Ettie and then Elsa-May. "What can I do for the two of you?"

"Ettie's come to apologize."

Ettie's mouth dropped open and she stared at Elsa-

May. She looked back at the detective. "We've both come to apologize to you—"

"What have you done now, Mrs. Smith?"

She could tell Elsa-May was stifling a giggle. "Stop it, Elsa-May. You wouldn't be like this if it was your daughter accused of murder." That wiped the smile off Elsa-May's face.

"What is it?" Kelly glanced at his watch. "You'll have to be quick."

"Ettie and I have come here to apologize for bringing Alice in to speak with you."

He raised his eyebrows. "Is that it?"

"Yes. She told us something very different and we thought she should tell you what she told us and then when she got here, she changed what she said."

"I can only go by what she said to me."

"And that's exactly why we've come to say that we're sorry we wasted your time."

Ettie added, "Yes. We didn't know she was going to change what she said. She said—"

Kelly raised his hand. "It doesn't matter what she said to you. It's interesting that she's been named in the will. When I heard you were bringing her in I thought she might open up can of worms."

"A can of worms?" Elsa-May asked.

"That's an expression. It means to bring something to light that adds confusion to the mix, perhaps something sinister, or something previously unthought-of of, or unheard of."

"I see."

"Well, apology accepted." He looked over at Ettie. "I know you're upset about your daughter, but just trust the process. If she's not guilty then she's got nothing to worry about."

"I wish that were true. Many a mistake has been made in the justice system. Look at all the people who've gone to jail and then years later it's been found out they were innocent."

"I've got no time for a debate." A tiny smile hinted around his lips. "if you don't trust the system, Ettie, trust me. I won't let that happen."

Ettie saw the detective's lips turn upward into a smile, but it was devoid of sincerity. "Thank you. We've taken up enough of your time." Ettie was halfway pushing herself up out of her seat when Detective Kelly spoke again.

"The good news is that Sparkle hasn't been accused of anything, not yet. She's in a very precarious position, however, with that bottle having been found in her house."

Elsa-May said, "Since Mrs. Carter told you all about the poison doesn't that point to her more than to Myra?"

Ettie sat back down. "Someone planted that bottle in Myra's house."

"I hear what you're saying and we're looking into all possibilities."

"Thank you," Ettie said as she got to her feet.

"You should know this by now, Mrs. Smith, that when there's a murder the people who fall under the most suspicion are those closest—the spouse in particular."

Ettie nodded. She felt a little better after hearing him say that.

CHAPTER 8

WHEN THE TAXI turned into Elsa-May and Ettie's street, they saw Ava's horse and buggy outside their house.

"Did you know Ava was coming?" Elsa-May asked Ettie, as they climbed out of the taxi.

"Nee, did you?"

Elsa-May shook her head.

The taxi zoomed away, and Ava got out of the buggy and walked over to them.

"Is anything wrong, or is this just a kind visit to a couple of old ladies?" Elsa-May asked her.

Ava giggled. "I haven't seen you for some time, so I thought I'd visit."

"Good." As Ettie pushed open the front door, she asked, "How's Jeremiah?"

"He's good. He's doing some more work on the house."

"More work?"

"Hasn't he finished it by now?" Ettie asked.

"*Jah,* most of it. He's doing some work on one of the bedrooms."

"Oh."

Once they were inside the house, Elsa-May asked, "Would you like tea?"

"*Jah,* you two sit. I'll get it."

While Ettie and Elsa-May sat down at the kitchen table, Ava got the tea ready. She looked over and said, "We thought it would be a good idea to get one of the bedrooms ready in case we have a visitor in a few months."

"That's nice. You never know when you're going to have unexpected visitors. Of course, we can't have any here because this place is too small," Elsa-May said.

"Florence stayed with us one time, but I had to sleep on the couch. It was most uncomfortable. Elsa-May snores, so that's why she couldn't sleep on the couch, so she said."

Elsa-May chuckled. "It's true. I didn't want to keep anyone awake."

Ava sat with them at the table waiting for the kettle to boil. "We're painting the walls a pale yellow, almost a cream because we don't know whether we might have a girl visitor or a boy visitor come to stay with us."

"Good idea."

Ettie agreed. "Neutral shades are always the best."

Ava smiled and nodded. "I forgot to tell you that,

while I was waiting to tell you my exciting news, Myra came and said she'd call back later."

Ettie leaned forward. "What did she say?"

"Just that she'd stop by tomorrow to see what you'd learned. She didn't tell me what it was about and I didn't feel like I should ask."

"We should tell her, Ettie."

"Tell me what?" Ava asked.

"Wait," Ettie said, "you've got exciting news, Ava?"

"She means about the room being painted, Ettie," Elsa-May said. Ava sighed and Elsa-May leaned over and patted her hand. "Don't worry. I get frustrated with Ettie sometimes too. Ettie, why don't you tell Ava all about what's happening with Sparkle?"

"Sparkle?" Ava gave Ettie a curious look.

Ettie rolled her eyes and then proceeded to tell Ava the whole story, including the Myra-to-Sparkle name change, and managed to finish just as the whistle of the kettle sounded.

"What can I do to help? I've always gotten along with Myra, um, I should say Sparkle, and I don't like to see the innocent accused."

"She hasn't been officially accused of anything yet."

Ettie said, "She's being set up. That's what it sounds like. There can be no other explanation if she's never seen that bottle before."

"That's right," Elsa-May said.

Ettie thought back to when Ava and Myra had last interacted. It was some time ago when they met in

Ettie's house. Ava was so much younger than Myra that they hadn't grown up together, and Myra had been out of the community for many years.

Elsa-May said, "If you can do anything, Ava, we'll let you know."

While Ava poured the tea, Ettie nibbled on a fingernail. Somehow, they had to find a way to meet Mrs. Carter and her son and ask them some questions.

"What's got you bothered, Ettie?" Elsa-May stared at her sister.

"I'm just wondering how we can find out more so we can help Myra...Sparkle. My daughter."

After Ava had placed their teacups in front of them, she sat back down. "I'll have to go as soon as I drink this tea. Tea always settles my stomach and lately when I've been cooking, I feel slightly sick with the smells of the food."

"That's too bad," Elsa-May said. "I hope you feel better soon."

"I think I'll get over it. It might take a few months, though."

Ettie said, "I'm sure you'll feel better before that. You must've caught some bug that's been going around."

"I'm sure that's all it is," Elsa-May agreed before she loudly slurped her tea.

"No, it's not a bug. And it's nothing I caught." Ava sighed once more.

"I just hope the detective hurries up and finds the killer," Ettie said.

Ava nodded. "I hope so too, for Myra's sake." She shook her head. "Sparkle's sake. This new-name business is hard to remember."

CHAPTER 9

THE NEXT MORNING, Elsa-May was taking a break from her knitting. She was cleaning the windows at the front of the house when Ettie heard her call out, "It's Detective Kelly and he's just pulled up and is getting out of his car."

Ettie looked up from washing the breakfast dishes and yelled back, "Is he smiling?"

"Is he ever?"

"Nee," Ettie said under her breath as she dried her hands on a tea towel. She heard the front door squeak open and went out to see if he had news.

He gave Ettie a nod after he had greeted Elsa-May. The look on his face told Ettie he had news, alright, but he didn't have any good news.

"You've got the results back from the toxicology?" Ettie asked.

"I have, I'm afraid."

"Was it poison you found in Myra's house?" Elsa-May asked.

"It was."

Ettie felt her knees going weak and moved to sit down on the couch while Elsa-May showed Kelly into their small living room. He sat down on a wooden chair opposite Ettie.

"We pushed through the results. They normally take longer than this, but this time we had the benefit of there being a label on the bottle. It's an extremely toxic substance. One drop on the skin can kill. Although, I'm told it might not be an instant death, but in some cases it could be."

"It was what it said? That poison with the long name?"

"Yes. That's right."

Ettie fought back tears. Myra had been framed, but how would she prove her innocence? They knew none of the people involved in this apart from Myra, and had just met Alice, the old housekeeper. Alice knew the family, but she hadn't been living amongst them for years, so she was of no real help.

"What does that mean for Myra?" Elsa-May asked.

Kelly blew out a deep breath. "The bottle didn't have her prints on it, but—"

"That's good then, isn't it?" Elsa-May asked.

"Not especially because there were no prints at all. The bottle had been wiped clean."

Ettie and Elsa-May stared at each other and then looked back at Kelly.

"Myra was set up—framed," said Ettie in a shaky voice. "Whoever planted it there wiped off the prints."

"As I said earlier, we're looking into every possibility, but so far we're drawing a blank every direction we turn."

Ettie was bitterly disappointed to hear that news.

"As Sparkle might have told you, we've taken her crystals for testing. We need to find if this substance is on any of her other crystals. We don't want more people dropping dead."

"Of course not. That would be dreadful."

"And when do you find that out?" Ettie asked.

"It's a very time-consuming and hazardous process, considering the toxicity of the substance we're dealing with."

Elsa-May leaned forward. "If you don't mind me asking, who did Ian leave his money to?"

"I'm afraid that's something I can't tell you at this stage."

"It wasn't Myra, was it?" Ettie asked.

"Ettie's right. Whoever he left the money to is obviously the guilty party," Elsa-May said.

A smirk twitched around Kelly's lips. "Interesting you should say that."

"Why's that?"

He shook his head. "I can't say. The official reading

of the will is on Friday, and Sparkle will be in attendance."

Ettie gasped. "You mean Sparkle was named in the will?"

"That would be obvious, wouldn't it? If she wasn't named in the will she wouldn't need to be there."

"She never mentioned anything to us," Ettie said.

"She might not have known when she last talked to you," Kelly said.

Ettie wished Elsa-May had never mentioned anything about the guilty party being left something in the will. Not that Kelly would listen to anything she said, but it sure wouldn't have helped, sending his thoughts in that direction.

He stood up. "Well, I just wanted to deliver that news to you in person."

"Thank you for taking time out of your day to come over and tell us."

Ettie nodded. "Yes. We appreciate that very much."

"It's no trouble. I was out this way."

Ettie stayed in her seat while Elsa-May showed Kelly to the door. When Elsa-May sat back down, Ettie said, "This is not good. It just isn't good. I'm sick to my stomach."

"I know, but don't panic just yet."

Elsa-May clasped her hands together. "Myra always gets herself into scrapes."

"We can't look back, we can only look forward."

"I know. Where do we go from here?" Ettie asked.

"Nowhere."

"What?"

"Where's Snowy?" Elsa-May looked over at the empty dog bed. "He might be outside?" While Ettie was still sitting there worrying about what was going to happen with Myra, Elsa-May looked in the backyard. "He's not out here either!"

"He didn't get outside when Kelly came here, did he?"

"The door was ajar when we showed Kelly out."

Ettie pushed herself up off the couch. "He must've sneaked out then. Quick, grab the lead we'll have to find him."

Elsa-May grabbed the leash from its hook behind the door and they walked down the porch steps calling and whistling to him.

"You go that way and I'll go this way," Elsa-May ordered.

"Look! There he is." Ettie saw the white dog darting about on the neighboring driveway. He stopped still, looked at them and then went toward the new neighbors' front door. Just as they were at the bottom of the neighbors' driveway, hurrying toward him, they saw Snowy lift his leg. He relieved himself on one of the five leather suitcases by the door.

"Did you see what your dog just did?" Ettie said, horrified.

"Oh dear. This isn't a good way to make friends with the new neighbors." Snowy scampered toward

Elsa-May and she leaned down and picked him up. "Naughty boy. What were you thinking?"

"You'll have to tell them what happened. Ask if they'll give us a rag and some water so we can clean it up."

"Right." Elsa-May walked forward and knocked on the door. She waited a while and then knocked again, this time a little louder. "No one's home."

Ettie produced an old handkerchief out of her sleeve. "Just as well this is an old one." She wet it from the outside tap, and then wiped the suitcase the best she could, moving it clear of the wet spot. "That will have to do."

Elsa-May clipped the leash onto Snowy's collar and then placed him down on the ground. "He's never done anything like this before."

"Not that we've seen. We'll have to keep a better eye on him."

"Normally, he's all over Detective Kelly, and this time he ignored him to slip out the door."

"Kelly's bad news and solemn face might have scared him."

"Maybe."

When they got Snowy safely back home, their thoughts turned again to Myra.

"Why don't we pay Myra a visit and see if there's anything that she's forgotten to tell us?" proposed Ettie.

"You mean something she's kept from us?"

"It's not unusual for friends to leave other friends

something in their wills, but I wonder if he was anything more than a client and a friend?"

"Mmm, I wondered that too, especially with Ronald out of the country." Elsa-May's eyebrows rose. "We know that's what the wife thought."

"Get your coat on. Let's see what she has to say now that we know Ian's left her something in his will."

CHAPTER 10

MYRA'S HOUSE was in a street full of nice houses and it fit in well. It was painted white with a gray-shingled roof, and in the front was a well-looked-after garden. Ettie had half expected her to live in something that looked like a medieval haunted castle, with gargoyles at the rooftop corners and huge lions protecting the front door. Possibly even a couple of crows flying overhead.

"It's nice, isn't it?" Ettie asked Elsa-May.

"*Jah.* It's lovely."

They walked through the gate of the white picket fence and up the sidewalk, and Elsa-May pressed the doorbell. Myra opened it and then unlocked the security screen standing between them.

"Come in."

Elsa-May looked Myra up and down as she walked in. "Sorry to catch you in your dressing gown, Myra."

Myra looked down at what she was wearing. "It's Sparkle, Aunt, and this isn't my dressing gown."

"Ach, jah, Sparkle." Elsa-May looked her up and down again. "Are you sure it's not a dressing gown?"

"Yes. This is a dress."

"You could wear it as a dressing gown if you wanted to."

"Thanks for the fashion advice, but I hope you don't get offended if I don't take it."

"Can we talk to you for a few minutes?" Ettie asked Myra, nudging Elsa-May out of the way.

"We're talking now, aren't we, Mother?"

"Ettie means, 'Can we sit down and talk?'" Elsa-May said.

"Fine." Myra walked further into the house, and called over her shoulder, "Come through to the sunroom."

They made their way down a long hallway full of strange paintings and posters, mostly of bald men sitting cross-legged meditating. At the end of the hallway was a light-filled room that overlooked the back garden.

Elsa-May and Ettie sat on a couch covered by a tassled throw. "You have a beautiful house, Sparkle."

"Thank you, Aunt. I like it. If you'll notice, there's lots of fresh air and light coming into this house. It's very different from your house, Mother. Your house has no ventilation and you keep those curtains closed all the time."

"If I have a breeze on me I start to cough."

Myra rolled her eyes. "I'm sure it's all in your head."

Elsa-May said, "The detective let slip to us that you're going to be at the reading of the will."

"Yes, I've only just found out myself. Ian's left me something. That was thoughtful."

"Do you have any idea what it is?" Ettie asked.

"No. I have to wait to find out. It won't be much because he had two sons and two wives. The wives act fairly friendly with each other, considering, but the will might end all that." Myra breathed out heavily. "I've got an idea he might have left me his crystal collection."

"According to the housekeeper—the old former housekeeper, Ian's first son also likes crystals."

Myra nodded. "That's true. He's a member of the society. Angelo and his father didn't get along, though. I truly think Ian would rather me have his collection."

"Why didn't they get along if they had the same interests?"

"That's all they had in common, from what Ian told me."

"Strange Ian would leave you something. I know you said he was a good friend, but is there any reason he'd—"

Sharply, Myra cut Ettie off. "All right, if you must know, there was a flirtation between us. Nothing more, but I have a sneaking suspicion that Ronald thought there was something more to it, and that's why he chose this time to chase up some loose ends with that old case."

"But Ian's a married man." Elsa-May's face scrunched into a sour expression.

"You can't help who you fall in love with, Aunt."

"*Jah,* you can. You jolly well can." Elsa-May's eyes bugged out.

Myra sighed. "Don't get your bloomers in a twist. I wasn't in love with him anyway. I was trying to make a point just now. It's hard talking to the both of you because you don't live in the real world. We were just friends, like I said before, but good friends. He liked me more than I liked him but it was a purely platonic relationship."

"Don't you see how bad this looks for you now, with you being named in the will?" Ettie asked.

"I can tell what it looks like and I can't do anything about it. I just want to be able to grieve alone without all this nonsense going on. I've done nothing wrong and I've had no time to be sad over losing a friend."

"Who, Crowley?" Elsa-May asked.

Ettie got in before Myra, and answered, "She means Ian."

"Why didn't you tell us how close you were to him?"

"I thought I did. I told you we sat and talked about our lives over green tea after his appointments were finished. Anyway, what does it matter? I'm a grown woman and I don't need a lecture."

"We're just worried about you and want the best for you, that's all," Elsa-May said.

Myra's bottom lip trembled and she hung her head. "I don't want to go to jail."

Ettie didn't know what to say to comfort her. It was sad that they weren't close, and if Myra went to jail, she'd waste away. That led Ettie to wonder if she had a good lawyer. With all her clients leaving her now that the news was out about her being suspected in Ian's death, did she need money? "And, how are you doing financially now?"

"I'm fine. I'm comfortable and don't need to work anymore, so it's neither here nor there that most of my clients have left me. It's affected my reputation, but not my lifestyle." Myra blinked rapidly and stared at the ceiling. "Perhaps all this has happened because my feng shui needs attending to."

"Your what?" Ettie asked.

"Never mind," Myra said weakly.

"I suppose the detective knows about your relationship with Ian?" Elsa-May asked.

"You make it sound so awful. We weren't having an affair or anything. Then again, if you want to get technical, it could've been classed as an emotional affair. We relied on each other for emotional support."

"What about Crowley? Didn't he emotionally support you?" Elsa-May asked.

"He doesn't understand my spirituality. He doesn't mind what I do with my crystal healing and so forth, but he just doesn't get it. Ian and I just clicked in that department. He recognized my gift."

"Your gift of crystal healing?" Elsa-May asked.

"That's right," Myra agreed.

Ettie shook her head, wondering how she could've produced such a daughter. "I wish we could've known all this in the first place," Ettie muttered.

"As I said before, it doesn't make any difference because I'm not guilty. I didn't kill him and I didn't give him a poisoned crystal to take home with him, or any crystal. Besides that, I only heal with double-terminated crystals and the one they showed me a photo of, that they said had the poison, wasn't even double terminated. I haven't seen that crystal before in my life."

"How would you remember all the crystals you've ever seen?" Ettie asked. "I'm assuming you would've seen quite a few."

"I have, and it's because that crystal had a particularly distinctive black tourmaline crystal in the center of it and a smaller one below it. I've got quartz crystals that have tourmaline crystals in them, but they're much smaller."

"I see," Elsa-May nodded. "Crystals can have other crystals inside them?"

"That's right. It happened millions of years ago when the molten rock started to cool."

"Interesting," Ettie said.

Myra jumped to her feet. "You should go. It was a mistake to ask you to help."

Ettie pushed herself to her feet. "We will help. You didn't kill the man, so we'll help."

Myra's face contorted and then she burst into tears.

CHAPTER 11

ETTIE SAT BACK DOWN, stunned, and Elsa-May moved over to comfort Myra by putting her arm around her. She guided Myra back to her seat, murmuring, "There, there. It's okay." Elsa-May sat back down, too. "It'll all work out. We're praying about you."

"Why do these things continue to happen to me? First, there was my husband who wasn't really my husband, well he was, but he had a fake name, and then ..."

Elsa-May raised her hand. "Things will work out."

"I don't know if they will. I can't understand why this is happening to me. Maybe it's Mercury retrograding. I should learn more about astrology because something's wrong. It's all just wrong."

"Mercury? The same name as the poison," Ettie said.

"Stop it, Ettie. It was only part of the name and

you're not helping. You know she's talking about the planet, Mercury."

Myra put her head up and sniffed. "Mercury was the Roman messenger to the gods. The planet was named after him, and I believe the chemical was named after the planet. Anyway, I wish I'd never heard of it."

"Have you tried praying about everything?" Ettie asked.

"Prayers are not based on fact. Let's face it, Mother."

"Is crystal healing?" Ettie shot back. "I know where I'd rather put my trust."

"God made the crystals. They're from the earth and He made the universe." Myra glared at her mother. "You've never understood me. Not many people do. I suppose it's not your fault, with how you were raised and all."

"That should make you feel even more pleased with Crowley," Elsa-May said.

Myra frowned at her aunt. "He never understood me, he just went along with whatever I said. I don't think that's a true soulmate experience."

"Maybe it is," Elsa-May said. "He loves you no matter what. Whether you're a crystal healer, whether you have a wellness center, or whatever you want to do."

Myra dabbed at her eyes. "I guess that's true. He's always been very accepting of whatever I want. I do like to experience different things and I have an open mind. He's supportive of me."

"Good men are hard to find, especially when you get older," Ettie said.

Myra laughed. "Have you been looking, Mother?"

Ettie chuckled. "No I haven't because it seems there are no men left that are my age."

Myra shuddered. "Thank goodness for that."

"I agree," Elsa-May said. "I don't fancy living with Ettie and her new husband. Snowy and I would have to move out somewhere else, into a different home."

Ettie suggested, "You could always stay at the house, and my new husband and I will move somewhere else."

Elsa-May shook her head. "I don't know what we're doing even talking about this because it's never going to happen."

Ettie chuckled again. "It makes me feel young again to think about it."

"That ship has sailed a long time ago, Mother. You're way too old to think about men." Myra shuddered again. "Anyway, back to the problem at hand. I'm in big trouble if more crystals come back with poison on them. If I had opened that bottle I could've died."

"You never ever saw the bottle?" Elsa-May asked.

"No, never. They told me they found it hidden at the back of a shelf in my pantry." Myra looked down at her hands in her lap.

Elsa-May said, "Tell us everything you know about the two wives and the two sons."

"That's a hard question. I know everything about them."

"Start with Angelo," Ettie said.

"I knew him before I met Ian. He was a client and then he suggested to his father that he come to me for treatment. I thought I told you that. We're members of some of the same groups."

"So, Ian got along better with son number one or number two?" Ettie asked.

"Well, he didn't talk about son number two much. He mostly complained about son number one, Angelo."

"Did Ian still get along with wife number one?" Elsa-May asked.

"Yes. He did, but not until after things calmed down from the divorce."

"What is the son from the second marriage like?"

"Ian didn't get on so much with Byron either at times. They were worlds apart in their views on things. Angelo and Bruno both worked in their father's company and neither wanted him to sell it. I'd reckon it's not so easy to work their way up the ladder if their father is not the owner of the company anymore. They both still work in the company now."

"Yes, I could see that might be a problem for them," Elsa-May said.

"Anyway, I'm sure Tiffany just married him for his money. That's what Ian thinks too. Well, that's what he thought." Myra jumped up when the phone sounded from another room. "Excuse me, that's the phone."

Ettie and Elsa-May sat there in silence while Myra

was gone. They couldn't hear what Myra said on the phone, they only heard her speak in a low tone. When she came back into the room, she sat down in front of them. "That was Ian's brother. Ian's body has been released and the funeral is on the day after tomorrow. The reading of the will is on the day after that at Ian's lawyer's office."

"Are you going to his funeral?"

Myra put her fingertips to her lips. "I don't even know what time it is. I will go if I can find out."

"Would you like me to go with you?" Ettie asked.

Myra's eyes glistened. "Would you?"

Elsa-May answered for Ettie, *"Jah,* if you'd like us to."

"That would be good. I need some support and I don't know when Ronald's coming home."

"You haven't told him about all this business yet?"

"No, I haven't."

"Don't you think you should?"

"I don't ... I don't want to alarm him. He doesn't do well under pressure."

That didn't sound like the Crowley Ettie knew. "I wouldn't say that's right."

"I know him better than anyone and I know he doesn't do well under pressure. He's changed since he left the force. Now he plays golf most days."

"What about his private detective business? Last time we saw him he was excited about it. Didn't he carry on with it?"

"Yes, he did. He doesn't get much work. He's only worked on a few cases."

"That surprises me. I thought he would've got a lot of work considering the high position he reached as a police officer … detective, I should say."

"He's offered a lot of work, but he declines most things. Knowing him, he probably only takes on the more complicated cases. All the ones that appealed to him in some manner. He's all about fairness and doesn't like to see people wronged."

"He always was a complicated man," Ettie said looking out at the peaceful garden through the glass doors. Two birds were splashing in a birdbath, and when a larger bird came the smaller birds flew away. It always filled Ettie's heart with happiness to watch birds at play.

"Complicated? I never thought so," said Elsa-May.

Ettie pulled her mind back to the problem. She looked at Elsa-May while wondering what to say to comfort her daughter. If she said the wrong thing it would make Myra feel worse than she already did.

Myra sniffed. "I still can't take it in that he's actually gone. He had expected to pass over to the other side from his heart condition, and he knew he had limited time. It's so much worse to go like this, though, before his natural time. He could've had another few months, maybe even a year."

"Yes, it is a shame," Ettie said.

"Thank you. I'll feel much better if you'll both be at the funeral."

Ettie was pleased that Myra felt that way. There was a spark of hope for their mother-daughter relationship.

"You know Ian's brother?"

"Yes. He had a couple of sessions with me to get over the loss of his wife. I don't think he thought it helped, because he only had those two sessions and then he cancelled the rest. Ian introduced us."

"How did his wife die?" Ettie asked.

"Car accident, not by poisoning. Don't start being suspicious of him. He wouldn't have done it."

"Why not?"

"Because they were close, more like twins than just brothers. Thanks for coming, but I've got a lot to do today. I have someone coming in half an hour for an appointment and I must prepare. I'll give you the address where the funeral will be." Myra jumped up and scribbled something in a book and then ripped out the page and handed it to them. "I'll let you know the time as soon as I can."

CHAPTER 12

Myra had stopped by yesterday to inform them of the time for the service, and she told Ettie and Elsa-May that she would meet them at the funeral. They had hoped that Myra would collect them in her car, but perhaps she would give them a ride home instead. It got costly going everywhere by taxi.

Ettie stepped out of the taxi and stared at the small church. It was all white except for the arched wooden double doors and the fancy stained-glass windows. "What a pretty church."

Elsa-May paid the driver, climbed out, and stood beside her. "It is indeed. Shall we sit at the back?"

"Jah. I'm sure Myra won't sit at the front considering the circumstances. I don't think Tiffany will be happy to see her here at all."

"Nee, she won't. I hope there isn't a scene. What

would you do if a woman you thought had murdered your husband came to his funeral?"

Ettie pushed her long bony finger into the air. "Ah, but Tiffany knows Myra didn't do it, and her lies about Myra prove that."

Elsa-May looked around, noticing there were other people arriving. "True, but she'd have to put on a show to make it look good. Perhaps we should talk about this at a different time?"

"Okay, you're right. Let's find Myra and get our seats." The two elderly sisters made their way through the tall double doors of the church and were immediately faced with the highly-polished wooden coffin standing on a raised platform at the front of the church. A large wreath of yellow roses nearly covered the top of the closed coffin.

They couldn't see Myra anywhere, so they sat in the last pew on the right-hand side. "I wonder if we're going to be too far at the back," Ettie said.

"It depends how many people come."

Ettie counted twenty rows of wooden pews. Looking toward the front of the church, to her left side were a stage and the pulpit, and to the right stood a large piano-style organ.

Elsa-May poked Ettie in the ribs. "Look, there's the second wife, Tiffany, I'll bet. She's fussing around with the flowers as if she owns the place.

Ettie looked at the woman repositioning the large yellow and gold floral arrangements situated at either side of the casket. "You mean the first wife or the second wife?"

"The very last Ian had, the second."

Ettie and Elsa-May sat back and watched people greet the woman they suspected was Tiffany. She was a small woman with platinum-blonde hair. A tall young man whispered something to Tiffany, and then they both stared at a well-dressed dark-haired woman approaching. The young man quickly took his seat.

The woman walked right up to Tiffany, and they smiled at one another and kissed each other on both cheeks.

"I'd guess that's Maria, the first wife."

"Did you see that, Ettie? The son from the second marriage doesn't like wife number one. And that young man over there looking none-too-happy came in with that woman, and he sat over there." Elsa-May nodded her head to show Ettie where she meant.

"Ah, so the dark-haired woman is Maria, and that over there is her son, Angelo."

"*Jah,* and both sons don't like the other wives."

"Hmm. I think you're right. Look at how different the two women are. Tiffany is blonde and small, whereas the first wife is tall with black hair."

"Black hair going gray," Elsa-May corrected.

"When he married her, she would've had black hair," Ettie said, trying to hide the annoyance at her older sister correcting everything she said.

While more people came in and found their seats,

Elsa-May whispered, "I suppose that doesn't mean anything. I mean, why would they?"

"Why would who do what?" Ettie asked.

"If your *vadder* left your *mudder* for another woman, would you get along with her?"

"Are we still talking about the sons?"

Elsa-May nodded. *"Jah."*

"That's not a fair question because that would never happen."

"A question can neither be fair or unfair. It's simply a question, Ettie."

"It might be a question, but it's a question we might never find the answer to if we can't get closer to these people." Ettie crossed her arms in front of her chest and stared straight ahead.

"Maybe the divorce was traumatic and that Tiffany woman was the cause of it. You never know."

Ettie leaned over and whispered, "We need to find out about the dynamics of all the relationships from Myra."

"She already told us what she knows. Look at them." Elsa-May nodded her head to the front of the church. "Are you surprised at the wives getting along?"

"Maybe they were divorced before Tiffany came into the picture." Ettie stared at the two women. She didn't trust Tiffany at all, not with all the lies she'd told about Myra. It was a good thing that Detective Kelly was cautious and not taking what Tiffany said too seriously. If he had, Myra might have been arrested by now.

"I don't really know." Elsa-May spoke absently as she watched the people filing through the doorway.

"I thought Myra would've been here by now. I hope she's all right."

"Stop fussing, Ettie. She'll be fine."

Ten minutes later, the ceremony started. Instead of the organ being played, music rang out through the speaker system. The two women Ettie and Elsa-May had figured were the wives sat with their respective sons at the front of the church on opposite sides of the center aisle.

After the song finished, a man got out of his seat and approached the microphone in front of the pulpit. He tapped on the microphone, and then cleared his throat. "I want to thank everybody for coming here today. For those of you who don't know me, I'm Ian's brother, John. He was my older brother." He paused for a moment as though he were fighting back tears, swallowed hard, and then continued, "Ian was a man of great vision. He started selling papers when he was nine…"

Elsa-May and Ettie sat and listened how Ian had started off as a paperboy, and then worked his way up in a company and then he eventually bought it, developed it, and improved it to the point that twenty years after he took it over, he sold it after it went public.

"Apart from that, he was a father, a husband, a son,

and a brother." John looked down trying to compose himself again.

"I wonder where Myra is," Elsa-May said a little too loudly; a lady two rows in front turned around and glared at her.

Embarrassed, Ettie dug Elsa-May in the ribs and frowned at her to keep quiet.

Ian's brother continued, "He will be missed greatly by all those who knew him. He was a philanthropist and gave his time to many—" John then looked up and stared open-mouthed, looking at the back door of the church.

Everyone turned and looked to see what had caused that reaction. It was Myra, dressed all in black. He was staring at her as she walked into the church. She found Ettie and Elsa-May and sat down with them. When Ian's brother started talking again, everybody turned back around except for Tiffany who was still glaring at Myra.

"Someone's not happy to see you," Ettie whispered.

"I know."

Then Ettie noticed Detective Kelly slip through the door and sit in the back of the church on the opposite side of the aisle from them.

Ettie dug Elsa-May in the ribs to notify her of Kelly's arrival. Elsa-May frowned at Ettie until Ettie tossed her head in Kelly's direction.

When John finished talking, the first son, Angelo, got up and said a few words about his father. He had a very low voice and to make it worse, he mumbled, making it hard for Ettie to understand what he said. When he sat down, a young girl got out of her seat, took the microphone and sang a song.

Myra leaned over and said to Ettie, "This was his favorite song."

"Who's that girl?" Ettie asked.

"One of his nieces. He often talked about what a good singer she was. Kelly's her name."

"You've met her?" Ettie asked.

"No, but he showed me her singing in a video on the Internet."

"Oh."

The second wife turned around and glared at Myra once more.

"She really doesn't like you," Ettie told Myra.

"I know. You can't half tell. It's a wonder she doesn't have security throw me out."

"Do they have security here?"

Myra rolled her eyes, and whispered, "It's just an expression, Mother."

"I see. I'd have thought so."

When the song finished, an elderly minister in black robes and a white collar said a few words about Ian's life and what a valued member of the church he'd been. Ettie looked at the crowd of people and wondered if the killer was sitting right there amongst them in one of the church pews. Detective Crowley had taught them that a murderer will often attend the funeral of the person they've killed. And that was most likely because the victim would have been killed by someone close to them.

Ettie gave a sidelong glance at Detective Kelly sitting there with one leg crossed over the other in his dark blue suit and black shiny shoes. He looked very well-presented, and better dressed than normal.

"What are you looking at?" Myra asked.

"Nothing." She looked back at the front with her mind lingering on Kelly's suits. He told her once that he never bought expensive suits because in his line of work he'd often have to wind up throwing them out. She didn't ask him why, but she guessed.

Ettie gave Detective Kelly another quick glance to see if he was looking at one particular person. Kelly caught her eye and gave her a tiny nod. She smiled and leaned back. He couldn't have thought Myra was guilty because she hadn't been arrested yet, but then again, they had gotten a search warrant and it wasn't good that they'd found the bottle of poison in her house. She knew that when someone was accused, it was hard to prove that they weren't guilty. It was hard to make a positive out of a negative.

CHAPTER 13

THE ATTENDEES at the funeral were told refreshments were being served in the room adjoining the church, and that afterward, only the family would attend a private burial ceremony.

Elsa-May leaned over and whispered to Ettie, "That's a bit cold. Mrs. Carter isn't even having people to her home."

"Because she doesn't want people like us there, no doubt," Ettie whispered back.

It made perfect sense to Ettie, because Tiffany was guilty. That explained why she was trying to throw suspicion off herself. She hoped the detective could see that. In Ettie's mind, it was as clear as a summer sky.

Before they left their seats, Myra told Ettie who was who. Two people had waved to Myra and they appeared friendly. Ettie guessed they might have been from the same crystal society as both Myra and Ian.

When Myra left the sisters to speak with other people, Ettie and Elsa-May followed the rest of the crowd into the other room for refreshments. The two sisters decided to keep their distance from the detective because they didn't want anyone to know that they knew him. Today was the best day to get around, mingle, and talk to a few of the people who had known Ian.

When they each had a cup of hot tea in their hands, Elsa-May said to Ettie, "You talk to Angelo, and I'll talk to Byron, and then we'll meet back here."

"Okay." Angelo was the first son, Ettie reminded herself. She saw him talking to a group of people and she hung back slightly. Then he moved away, heading to the refreshment table. She hurried over. "Angelo."

He turned around. "Hello."

"Hello."

"Did you know my father?" he asked.

"I knew of him and I just wanted to offer you my condolences."

"Thank you. That's very kind. How did you know him?"

"He was a friend of a friend."

"Thank you. It was nice of you to come." He gave her a polite nod, smiled and went to move on.

Ettie could not let him get away before she had learned something from him. She bit her lip, cranky with herself for not thinking of something before she approached him. "I understand you were young when your mother and father divorced?"

He stopped and turned around to face her. "That's right. The divorce happened when I was just a young child. I barely remember my mother and father being together."

"I couldn't help but notice that your mother and Tiffany don't quite get along, even though they're polite to each other." She hoped she wasn't being too nosey but she had to probe.

He smiled. "You're not a fan of Tiffany's?"

Ettie shook her head, hoping that was the way she could get through to him. "Not one bit."

He grinned. "It's not surprising. Not many people like her. I guess, neither did my father after some time, but it was too late by the time he realized it."

"Too late?"

"For a divorce. There was no prenup, that's what he told me. After the pay-out, he had to give Mom, he said he would be ruined if he had to divorce again." He gave her a little smile and then said, "If you'll excuse me, I'm ravenous. I had a big night last night and I'm still a bit hung over." He walked over to the table that was filled with small sandwiches and cupcakes.

Ettie was pleased she had gleaned a small amount of information from him. When Ettie turned around intending to locate Elsa-May, she was standing right in front of her.

"Well?" Elsa-May asked.

"Ian didn't get along with the second wife but couldn't divorce her because she would have taken most of the money. Also, I learned that Angelo doesn't particularly like Tiffany and is of the opinion that no one else much likes her either. What did you find out?"

"I think Byron's hiding something."

"What did he say?"

"He doesn't think that Myra did it. He thinks his father did away with himself because he was dying of heart disease."

Ettie frowned. "That doesn't make sense. I'm sure there was a far more efficient way for him to kill himself than poisoning. Especially so dangerous a poison."

"You're probably right. I'd reckon Byron had something to do with it." Elsa-May turned slightly, glancing in Byron's direction.

Ettie turned around and stared directly at Byron. "I suppose Tiffany will be left most of the money?"

"Most likely. We'll have to wait until tomorrow to find out for certain. I noticed Alice didn't come."

Looking around, Ettie said, "No she didn't, but I didn't think she would. Not with Mrs. Carter accusing her of stealing."

Ettie looked around for Angelo once more; he was with a group of people and then she saw him smile. Following his eyes, she saw he was smiling at Tiffany who smiled back. So! They did get along, even though he had made out to her that no one liked Tiffany, himself included. Ettie filed that away in her brain. She left Elsa-May and found John, Ian's brother. "I'm so sorry about your brother."

"Thank you. You were a friend?"

Ettie nodded. "In a roundabout way. Those were lovely words you said about him."

He smiled. "Thank you. It's hard to know what to say. There was so much more I could've said."

"It was dreadful for him to go in that way."

"It was such a shock to find out how he'd died."

"Do the police know who did it yet?"

Ettie noticed that John's eyes flickered to Tiffany who was talking to her son. "Not yet. If they have suspects they didn't mention anything like that to me. How did you know Ian?"

"Through a friend. It was nice to talk with you."

"You too."

Ettie made her way back to Elsa-May with a strong hunch that John thought Tiffany, or her son, Byron, was guilty.

Ten minutes later, Ettie and Elsa-May were joined by Myra. "Ready to go?"

"Yes," Elsa-May said.

"I'll drive you home."

"Denke, Myra." When Myra glared at Ettie, she corrected herself. "I mean Sparkle."

"Everyone here knows me as Sparkle, Mother."

"Yes, I'm sorry. It's hard for a mother to make that kind of a change."

"Come along. Are you ready?"

Ettie nodded. "I am."

Myra drove them home and Elsa-May talked her into coming in for a cup of tea.

A moment after Myra left Ettie and Elsa-May's house, a loud knock sounded on their door. "She's forgotten something," Elsa-May said, "I wonder who she takes after with that?"

"She certainly doesn't take after me. Or her *vadder*." Ettie opened the door and instead of Myra, she faced a stern-looking bald fifty-ish man with flushed chubby cheeks. She recognized him. He was their new neighbor, the man who'd moved in next door. Ettie had seen him moving packages from a truck into the house. Then she remembered what Snowy had done on one of his suitcases. He didn't look happy. Was that why he was there, because of Snowy?

CHAPTER 14

ETTIE FELT her heart start racing and she tried to steady her breathing as the man from next door loomed over her in her doorway. "Hello it's nice to meet you, I'm—"

"Look, Lady, your dog's been barking all day."

Ettie was shocked by his outburst. "I don't think that's right. He doesn't bark. He never barks."

Elsa-May was suddenly by her shoulder. "That's right, he never barks."

"He was barking non-stop and my wife had a headache all day. All that barking made it much worse. She was trying to sleep and she couldn't."

Snowy got off his bed and walked past Ettie and Elsa-May and sniffed the man's shoe.

The man kicked out at him. "Get,"

"Don't. He's harmless." Elsa-May said as she leaned down to pick Snowy up.

"Make sure you keep that dog away from us."

"You don't like dogs?" Ettie asked.

"Not ones that bark all day."

"Like we both said, he never barks. It must've been a different dog you heard."

"Is that right?"

"It is."

He placed his hands on his hips. "Where were you today?"

"We were out," Ettie said.

"Exactly." He pointed at Snowy. "And that dog was barking all day. Barking might be the wrong word. It was more of a high-pitched yapping, and if you don't shut it up, I'll get animal services to have it put down."

Elsa-May gasped and took a step back, hugging Snowy to her chest.

Ettie stood there with her mouth open. They'd never had a neighbor like him before and she didn't know what to say. All she could do was stare at him until he took a couple of steps back.

The neighbor then stomped away and yelled over his shoulder, "Just keep the thing quiet or else."

Ettie stared at Elsa-May. "Well, what do you think of that?" She closed the door.

"Do you think he barks?"

"I've only heard him bark once or twice in his whole life. And he didn't go on and on. It was just a couple little barks before he was quiet again."

Elsa-May nodded. "Every time we go out, I thought he just went to his dog bed and went to sleep."

"That's right. He sleeps most of the day and with the dog door he can go in and out as he pleases. What reason would he have to bark?"

Ettie closed the door. "That man didn't even tell us his name."

Elsa-May put Snowy down on the floor and he scampered back to his dog bed in the corner.

"I couldn't even confess what Snowy did to his suit-case." Ettie put her hand over her mouth and giggled.

Elsa-May laughed along with her. *"Nee,* it definitely was not the right time to confess about that."

"What will we do about Snowy? At least, we don't have to go home tomorrow. I mean, leave home," Ettie said.

"That's right. It's the reading at the will and we have to stay here until Myra comes afterward and tells us who the beneficiaries are."

"I do hope Myra wasn't left too much. She doesn't need money and it will make her look guilty." Ettie sat down on her couch, while Elsa-May sat down in her armchair.

"Do you still want to bake the neighbors a pie?" Elsa-May asked with a gleam in her eye.

"Jah. That might be just the thing. I'll take them a pie and do my best to win them over. And, might I remind you that you were going to bake the pie?"

Elsa-May breathed out heavily. "I'll do it, but I'm not going with you when you take it over to them. I'll stay home and protect Snowy."

Ettie chuckled and looked down at Snowy, who was back in his bed in the corner. "Snowy, were you barking all day?"

Snowy didn't move, he just looked at Ettie and his ears moved a fraction when he heard his name.

"What did Snowy say?" Elsa-May asked.

"He said he didn't."

Elsa-May chortled. "He must have. Otherwise, why would that man come over here complaining about it?"

Ettie bit her lip. "I don't know, but I sincerely doubt he barked all day like the man said."

Elsa-May picked up her knitting from the bag by her feet. "You might be right, Ettie."

"I usually am."

After shaking her head at her sister, Elsa-May popped her glasses onto the end of her nose and proceeded with her knitting, making that clickety-clicking noise with the needles that grated on Ettie's nerves. Today, that noise was the least of Ettie's problems.

CHAPTER 15

ETTIE AND ELSA-MAY waited as patiently as they could for Myra, and at three in the afternoon, Ettie saw Myra pull up in her bright red car. "Here she is," she called out to Elsa-May.

Elsa-May was just getting the second pie out of the oven. "Coming," she yelled out.

Ettie flung the door open and Myra rushed inside and sat down on the couch. It didn't escape Ettie's notice that, like at the funeral, Myra had worn all black to the reading of the will. Her dress was sleeveless with a high neckline and it looked far better than her usual flowing robes. Ettie sat beside her while Elsa-May sat on her usual chair.

"Well, what's the news?" Ettie asked.

"I knew Ian was wealthy, but I didn't realize how many millions he had." Myra sat and fanned herself with something.

"What's that you've got there?" Elsa-May asked.

Myra stopped fanning herself and looked at the papers in her hand. "This is the program, the order of service, from Ian's funeral. I had it in the car from the other day."

Elsa-May leaned forward and stretched out her hand and Myra gave it to her. "We didn't get one of these, Ettie."

Myra said, "They were on a table just as you went in the church doors. Have that one if you want."

As she looked at it, Elsa-May shook her head.

"I thought it odd that Tiffany didn't have people back to her home." Ettie didn't think the house had looked that grand for someone who had so much money, but she couldn't mention that because Myra would know they'd been snooping around Ian's house.

"People don't always do that," Elsa-May pointed out. "The last couple of funerals we've been to have been like that. Anyway, what did he leave you, Myra?"

"Jah, we've been waiting all day to find out."

"He left me his entire crystal collection."

Elsa-May's eyes grew wide. "Is that it?"

"Yes, he had some rare and lovely crystals. He knew that would've meant a lot to me, and it does."

"Go on," Ettie urged. "Who was left what?"

"His wife was surprised I wasn't left money. I could see that on her face. Surprised, but no doubt pleased."

"Tiffany?" Elsa-May asked.

"Yes. Tiffany was left more than half of the money

and then his first wife got nearly as much and the two sons got nothing. There were former employees left some small amounts of money, too."

"That's odd, isn't it, that the sons got nothing?" Ettie asked.

Myra shrugged. "I suppose he figured that the wives would then go on to leave the money to each son."

"I'd reckon that was a surprise to the sons, wasn't it?"

"They weren't there," Myra said. "Oh, and is someone moving out next door?"

"The old man moved out and new people have already moved in."

"That explains the moving truck."

"Another one? I don't know where they're putting all that furniture in such a small house." Ettie got up and peered out the window to see another moving company truck. This one was smaller than the last.

"It's a little bigger than this house," Elsa-May told Myra. "Your mother made me bake them a pie."

"That's nice of you, Mother."

Ettie's face lit up as she sat back down. "It's only the neighborly thing to do."

"They're not—"

Ettie had to interrupt her sister. "Mm ... Sparkle's not here to listen all about the neighbors today, Elsa-May."

"That's right. I don't like neighbors. I never talk to mine unless I have to. Otherwise, they'd come over all the time. That's what happens if you're too friendly. We have drinks in the street on Christmas Eve. That's quite enough for me."

"Somehow, I don't think we're going to have the problem of them coming over here all the time," Elsa-May said. "How many millions are we talking about, Mmm, um, Sparkle?"

Myra drew in a deep breath. "Fifteen million. Mostly in company shares. And a few million in change, in his bank accounts and such."

"Fifteen?" Ettie screeched.

"'And a few million in change,' you said?" Elsa-May asked.

"That's right. And I'm glad he didn't leave me any of it."

"Me too, or you might've been arrested," Ettie said.

"I'm not in the clear yet. Don't forget they found that poison in my house. Can you do anything to clear my name, do you think, Mother?"

"We're working on it," Elsa-May said.

Myra bounded to her feet. "I will appreciate anything you can do for me. I should go now. This has all been very stressful. I need to go home so I can unwind."

"I suppose you're going to meditate now to alleviate the stress?" Elsa-May asked.

"Something like that, Aunt. Is that the pie I can smell?"

"That's the pie I baked for the neighbors. I made

two. Would you like to take one with you?" Elsa-May asked.

"Thanks all the same, but no. Another time maybe."

They walked Myra to the door. Once she had gone, they returned to their usual seats in the living room.

Ettie sighed with relief. "That went well. She was only left the crystal collection."

"We should pay the detective another visit tomorrow."

"And why don't we leave Snowy with Ava while we do that?"

"Better still, she can drive us there and keep Snowy in the buggy while we talk to the detective."

"Good idea. You get the pie ready to take to the neighbors while I go down to the phone and call Ava to see if she's free tomorrow."

"Okay."

CHAPTER 16

WHEN ETTIE GOT BACK to the house after arranging their trip with Ava, Elsa-May had the pie wrapped in a tea towel. "Are you all set to go?"

"As ready as I'll ever be."

The two sisters closed the front door behind them and walked to the house next door. As they approach the front door, Ettie said, "It's very quiet."

"That must be how they like it."

Ettie stepped back a little way and allowed Elsa-May to knock on the door. She knocked three times and then waited a good four minutes before she knocked again. Then a woman that Ettie had already identified as the other new owner, apparently married to the bald man, slowly opened the door. She was a small skinny woman with curly dark hair and brown eyes.

"Yes?" she asked as she looked them up and down. There was no hint of a smile on her face.

"Hello, I'm Elsa-May and this is my sister Ettie. We live next door."

"The dog barking house?"

"Well, your husband visited us recently and mentioned that our dog was barking. We're very sorry about that."

She nodded. "As long as it doesn't happen again."

Ettie nudged her sister in the ribs, prompting Elsa-May to hold the pie out. "We baked you a pie."

When her eyes fell to the pie, her face softened and she opened the door a little wider. "How kind. Would you like to come inside?"

"We don't mind if we do," Ettie said and then bit her tongue. It was a strange thing to say, but the woman didn't seem to notice. At least she was smiling now.

"I'm Stacey and my husband's Greville. How about I make us a cup of hot tea?"

Ettie was worried that the husband would come back and throw them out. "We can't stay long, but thank you for asking."

"Can you at least sit for a moment?"

"Of course," Elsa-May said as she followed Ettie through the door.

Stacey led them through to the living room.

Once they were seated, Ettie asked, "What brings you to our nice little town?"

"We needed a change of scene and somewhere quieter."

"It is quiet around here. I'm sorry about the dog barking," Ettie said.

"It didn't really bother me. He only barked a few times, and he is a dog, after all. You have to forgive my husband. He's like a bear with a sore head sometimes."

"Is he at work now?" Ettie asked, hoping he wasn't in the house somewhere.

"Yes. He finishes at six."

Ettie's eyes traveled to the clock on the wall to see that it was already five thirty. They would have to leave soon to be sure they were gone before he got home. "And is it just the two of you living here?" Ettie asked.

"Yes, just the two of us. We don't have any children, sadly. And is it just the two of you living next door?" Stacey asked.

"That's right. Ettie and I are widows. Both of our husbands died many years ago and we sold our farms and moved in together."

"I've never met any Amish people before. This place is on the edge of the Amish community and we thought it would be peaceful and more out of the way from the hustle and bustle that we're trying to escape from."

"It is fairly quiet I suppose. We have a few other Amish people living on the street. Only one or two of us."

"Three households on the street, including ourselves," Elsa-May corrected Ettie.

"You're very kind to bring me pie. I haven't seen much kindness over the last few years."

"Really? Why is that?" Elsa-May asked.

"My husband doesn't like it when I leave the house or have friends visit. That's why my friends have stopped coming to see me."

"What is his reasoning for that?" Elsa-May's head tilted to one side.

"He's always been jealous and suspicious of me. I hope you didn't hear him yelling last night at a late hour?"

"If it was late, we would've both been asleep," Ettie said, feeling bad for the woman. Did she mean her husband was yelling at her?

"Oh," the woman looked down, appearing quite sad and embarrassed.

Ettie felt sorry for her, being married to such an angry man. And then she noticed Elsa-May glance at the clock. Then Ettie became worried that Greville might come home early and see the two of them there. He wouldn't be happy with them being there if his wife wasn't even allowed to have her own friends visit. "We should go," Ettie said.

"Already?" Stacey asked.

"Yes." Elsa-May nodded.

"Thanks for the pie and thanks for coming to see me."

"If you ever need anything we're not far away," Elsa-May said.

A smile met Stacey's lips and she nodded.

Ettie rose to her feet. "I'm glad you've got over that migraine."

Stacey frowned slightly, and then said, "Oh yes, thank you. I do get them from time to time."

When they reached the door, Greville loomed before them. Ettie jumped with fright at the sight of him. He glared at them and then offered his wife a filthy stare. He stepped back out of the doorway to allow them to pass.

"Our neighbors just brought us a pie," they heard Stacey say as he shut the front door with a thud. He hadn't even given Stacey a proper chance to say goodbye to them.

"We don't need pie. We need them to stop that dog yapping. Was it yapping again today?"

"No, not all."

Elsa-May had stopped still to listen, and Ettie took her arm and pulled her away. "That was horrible, Ettie. Did you see how cranky he looked with us?"

"I did. It was dreadful. He was even crankier with poor Stacey. He'll probably make her throw the pie out now." Ettie put her arm through Elsa-May's and together they walked down the driveway.

"How old do you think she is? I'd guess only in her early forties."

"Or a very well preserved fifty," Ettie said.

"It also occurred to me that the husband asked her if the dog had been barking again, which means that she must've told her husband about the barking in the first place. It's my guess she told him she was sick and the dog was barking all day and made her feel worse."

"What's your point, Elsa-May?"

"Well, it would be no wonder he was angry with us."

"Ah, so you think she told him lies about Snowy barking?"

Elsa-May nodded. "It's possible. Or at least exaggerations."

"For attention?"

They pushed their front door open. "Maybe," Elsa-May said, "She just gave me an odd feeling, and Granville, or Greville, or whatever his name was, scared me."

"Hmm. Not the neighbors we were hoping for."

"Not at all. I think I'll put the kettle on before I prepare the evening meal."

"Good. I feel like a hot tea right now since we didn't get one at our neighbors' place.

Elsa-May placed the teakettle on the stove and sat down at the kitchen table in front of Ettie. "I'm afraid there's nothing we can really do to help Stacey."

"I know. Not when we have Myra's problems to resolve."

Elsa-May nodded. "That's true, exactly what I was thinking."

CHAPTER 17

ETTIE AND ELSA-MAY had just sat down after washing up the dinner dishes when there was a knock on the door. Ettie's heart nearly stopped. "I hope that's not Greville." Snowy barked and Ettie immediately picked him up and closed him in Elsa-May's bedroom.

"I doubt it's Greville. If he had anything to say he would've said it earlier." Elsa-May got up to open the door. It was Detective Kelly. "Come in and sit down. Would you like a cup of coffee?"

"No thank you." He looked over at Ettie and she knew immediately that something was wrong.

"What is it?" Ettie's hand flew to cover her mouth.

"I'm afraid I've had to arrest your daughter, Mrs. Smith."

Ettie moved her hand to her chest. "Why?"

"There's a matter of the poison and now she also has motive."

"But how ... how did she have the motive? She told us she was only left the crystal collection. Was there more?"

"Why don't we sit?" Elsa-May said, guiding her sister to the couch.

Once they were all seated, Kelly explained, "In that crystal collection was the most valuable thing of all. It was an uncut rare blue diamond." He added, "Gem quality, internally flawless, I'm told."

Ettie and Elsa-May stared at one another, and then Ettie asked, "Myra didn't know?"

"That's what she claims, but why wouldn't she know if she knew his crystal collection? She claims she was a good friend and knew the man very well." Detective Kelly wiggled his eyebrows as if to let them know Myra's relationship with the deceased might have been more than client and practitioner.

"Where is Myra at the moment?" Elsa-May asked.

"In custody."

Ettie gasped when the reality hit her. "In jail?"

He nodded. "She should get bail in the morning."

"This is just awful," Ettie said. "Can I talk to her or see her?"

"Not until she's out on bail. Don't worry, she already has a lawyer, and she'll go before the judge in the morning. The judge will decide whether she may get bailed out or not. I would be very surprised if she was denied bail since there are no direct witnesses to the crime."

"She knew nothing about that crystal. She visited us directly after the reading of the will and was so pleased that she wasn't left anything of monetary value."

"Pleased she wasn't left anything?" he asked.

"Yes, and that way she thought people would realize she wasn't guilty. She didn't think the crystal collection was of much value."

Kelly pressed his lips together. "It sounds very much like something a guilty person would say."

"But she wouldn't have had a motive," Elsa-May said. "because she didn't know about the will or the diamond crystal."

"According to the wife, Ian and Sparkle were having an affair. Jealousy is a strong motive."

"They weren't having an affair. And she's the one who pointed the finger at Myra in the first place. She lied about Myra and Ian plotting to kill her. It's all lies. Can't you see that?"

He scratched his cheek. "How do you know?"

"Because Myra said so," Ettie said.

"Does she always tell you the truth?"

"Yes, she does. I raised her well. She might be a lot of things but she's not a liar."

The detective chuckled. "You can't have raised her as well as you'd hoped, I'm sure."

Elsa-May butted in. "Why do you say that?"

"Because she'd be Amish and married with eight children by now, wouldn't she?" Kelly smirked and appeared pleased with himself.

Under the circumstances, Ettie thought it was a cruel thing to say. "Everyone has to follow their own individual path. Myra has followed hers and that has been her choice."

"She's no killer," Elsa-May said.

Ettie was pleased with her sister for backing her up so vehemently. "Where did you say Myra is right now? In your station's jail or somewhere else?"

"At my station, but don't even try to see her. It's forbidden for anyone to visit after an arrest and before appearing before the judge and requesting bail. Except, those arrested are allowed to talk to their lawyers, of course. Oh, and your friend got a few stamps."

"Our friend?"

"Alice, the housekeeper. She inherited a meagre stamp collection." Detective Kelly put a comforting hand on Ettie's shoulder. "Put it out of your mind and I'll talk to you tomorrow." He got up and walked to the door.

Ettie stood and followed him. "How can I put something like that out of my mind?"

Elsa-May slipped her arm through Ettie's. Ettie felt sick to her stomach and couldn't even look at the detective who had arrested her daughter on a flimsy charge. When he had gone, Elsa-May closed the door.

Ettie let Snowy out of the bedroom and he scampered out the door sniffing all over the living room. Snowy had a liking for Kelly, but the feeling was not mutual. Elsa-May led her through to the kitchen and

Ettie sat down at the table while Elsa-May filled the teakettle with water.

"What you need is a cup of good strong tea and some cookies."

"What I need is a good sleep and I doubt I'll get that tonight."

"Neither of us will."

Nothing would stop Elsa-May from sleeping. Ettie knew she'd be snoring loudly in no time at all, keeping both herself and Snowy awake. "Myra didn't know about that crystal. It was obvious the way she was telling us that she was relieved that she only got his crystal collection. Had she known there was something valuable in there, she wouldn't have been so happy."

"I know. We both know Myra didn't do it and now we have to somehow convince the detective of that."

"We need some kind of a plan."

"Something will come to us, don't worry," Elsa-May said.

CHAPTER 18

EARLY THE NEXT morning they opened the door to Ava. She was to be driving them to talk to the detective that morning.

"Ava, we're so sorry. So much has gone on and we forgot you were coming today."

"You don't need to see the detective today?" she asked.

"He was here last night," Ettie said.

They sat Ava down in the kitchen and Ettie gave her the update on Myra and her arrest.

"I'm so sorry, that's awful."

"Would you like *kaffe?*"

"Nee denke."

"Tea?"

"Jah, please, weak and black."

While Elsa-May set about making the tea, Ettie moved closer to Ava and stared into her face. "Pale, dark circles under your eyes and instead of coffee, you're having tea... You're pregnant!"

Ava covered her mouth and giggled.

Elsa-May abruptly put the teakettle back down on the stove and turned around. "Are you?"

Ava nodded.

"Why didn't you tell us?" Ettie asked.

"Well I ... I wanted you to guess."

Ettie leaned over and hugged Ava.

"You can't keep anything from us, Ava. You should know that by now, what with Ettie's keen nose for finding things out." Elsa-May then embraced Ava. "You're finally expecting after all these years of marriage. How exciting!"

"It's only been about two years, hasn't it?" Ettie asked.

"*Jah.*" Ava nodded.

"Jeremiah must be out of his mind with joy."

"He is. We told his parents last night, and we were going to have you over for dinner, but I couldn't wait to tell you. I tried to give enough hints to you last time I was here, but ... can you come for dinner on the last Friday night of this month?"

"*Jah,* of course we can. This *boppli* will be my newest great grandchild, and your great grandniece, Ettie."

"I'm four and a half months along. Early on, I had morning sickness, but I'm fine now, just very tired. Jeremiah and I don't care whether it's a girl or a boy as long as ..."

"Everything will go well, Ava. Don't worry about a thing."

She nodded. "I know it."

Elsa-May moved over and placed a hand over Ava's stomach.

Ava squirmed and laughed. "There's nothing to feel yet. It's too early. I can feel movements, but I don't think you will."

"I'm just saying hello." Elsa-May grinned.

Ettie and Elsa-May passed a few relaxing hours with Ava and soon after she left, Myra arrived. Ettie and Elsa-May watched her walk up the steps.

"You got bail?" Ettie asked.

"Obviously."

"Come in." As soon as she walked in the door, Elsa-May said, "Kelly told us about the diamond."

Myra shook her head. "I never knew about that diamond. That wasn't any part of the crystal collection that I knew about. It was there in the list that the lawyer gave me on the day he read out Ian's will, but I didn't know it was going to end up being so valuable."

"Where is it now?"

"The police have it, along with the other crystals. Now they have my entire collection and Ian's. Even my own precious personal crystals that I would always have beside me when I sleep at night. What's your plan to get me off? I hope you have one."

Ettie wished she had a plan to get her daughter off,

but right now things didn't look too good. "I don't know yet. Who do you think did it?"

"The wife."

"Second or first?" Elsa-May asked.

Myra shot back, "The second one, Tiffany. I've always known she did it. Detective Kelly got in touch with Ronald and he's flying back tonight."

"That is good news," Ettie said.

"I don't know. I didn't want him to get mixed up in all this."

"Why not?" Ettie asked.

"Because it's such a dreadful business. He was a detective for so many years and now with me, his girl-friend, being accused of murder, it must be horrible for him."

"Have you spoken to him about it?"

"Briefly. This morning when he was waiting at the airport to board the plane. He said he'd sort it all out once he got back. I hope there's something he can do."

"There will be. He can investigate the wife and find holes in her story and that kind of thing."

Elsa-May agreed, "*Jah,* and we can't do things like that on our own."

"We need to find out who got into your house and put the poison there. It would've been good if you had some kind of surveillance security system."

"I don't."

"What about your neighbors?" Elsa-May asked.

"Even if they did, I don't know when that poison

would've been placed there. It was found in the back of one of my cupboards. It could have been there for years, or months. I can't ask the neighbors to look at a year's worth of their footage. Besides that, even if they have security cameras they might not have picked up any areas of my house."

"We need to find out where someone would have got that poison from," Ettie said.

"I'll try to find out."

"Haven't the police said anything?" Elsa-May asked.

"Not to me. Wait a minute." Myra pulled out a cell phone before the sisters could ask her to use it outside the house. She tapped on it a couple of times and then looked up at them. "It's for sale on the Internet. Anyone could've bought it, but they would've had to know what they were doing. It's highly toxic, even just the fumes, and it can eat through gloves."

Elsa-May sighed. "I was hoping it would be difficult to obtain."

Myra put the phone away. "Can someone make me a cup of coffee?"

Elsa-May pushed herself up off the chair. Once Ettie was alone with her daughter, she said, "I'm so sorry this is all happening to you."

"Why are you sorry?"

Ettie was taken aback. "I hate to see anything bad happening to you."

"Do you?"

Ettie stared at her daughter, seeing the pain and

hurt in her eyes. "Why are you so hostile with me all the time? Don't you know I love you? You're my child forever."

"I'm sorry. I love you too, Mother. I'm just stressed and it's not as though we've ever gotten along."

"We could if we both try."

"No, I don't think we ever could. We never did and we're just too different."

Ettie was still pleased that Myra had come to her in times of trouble. There must've been some kind of a bond there somewhere. "I hope we'll be able to get along better one day."

"Me too." Myra smiled. "The two of us are just so different. Like black and white, up and down."

"Fat and thin," Ettie said with a laugh.

Myra stared at her, and then jumped to her feet. "That's it!"

"What's it?" Elsa-May asked, having just walked back into the living room with a mug of coffee.

"Ian kept a list of everything he ate. Because of his heart condition his doctor told him he had to be under a certain weight. He was exercising as well and he just couldn't possibly still have been as overweight as he was. I think she was deliberately slipping fat into his food somewhere to keep him overweight."

"Maybe she was. That would be hard to prove, though," Ettie said.

Myra sat back down. "I guess you're right. It would be practically impossible to prove. And if somehow, they were able to prove that he did eat fatty foods, who's to say that he didn't cheat and eat them himself?"

Ettie said, "*Jah,* he could've had a burger or two on the quiet. It's very difficult to be so restricted all of the time."

Myra accepted the mug of coffee from Elsa-May, who then sat back down.

"Where do we go from here? If Tiffany is guilty how do we go about proving it?" Elsa-May asked.

"And was she the same person who put that bottle in your house?"

"I've been thinking about that. I had people from the crystal society to my house, and my clients come to the house for treatment. I suppose any one of them could've slipped the poison into the cupboard. Tiffany could've paid someone to do it."

"Someone you know?"

Myra nodded. "Quite possibly. Well, I think I'll go home and wallow in my misery there."

"Are you sure you don't want to stay awhile?"

"No, I'll be fine. I think better when I'm alone and Ronald will soon be there."

When Myra left, Ettie had an idea. "We all think Tiffany's guilty, so we need to pay a visit to her boutique."

Elsa-May giggled. "Us at a boutique?"

"Why not?"

"Why would we say we were there?" She picked up the end of her dress. "We won't find anything like this there and we'll stick out like two sore thumbs." Elsa-May dropped her dress.

"We can be just passing by and then if she's there, we'll recognize her from the funeral and then we'll go in and speak with her," Ettie said.

"She might not remember us. We didn't speak with Ian's wives, only his sons."

"No matter."

Elsa-May sighed. "Doing things like this is so awkward."

"I didn't say it would be fun, but we need to do something."

"Why? It's not as though she's going to confess to us."

"We'll find out more by trying to do something than we will by sitting here in the *haus* on our backsides."

Elsa-May nodded. "I guess you're right."

"Pardon?" Ettie leaned forward and held her hand up to her ear.

"I said, I guess you might be right, but it remains to be seen. The proof will be in the pudding."

"Pudding. Mmm that makes me hungry."

"We've only just had breakfast."

"I'd still like some pudding."

Elsa-May shook her head and started knitting. "It baffles me how you never gain weight."

"I'm naturally thin. I can eat anything—"

"All right, all right. Enough said."

"Why are you knitting?"

Elsa-May stopped and looked up at Ettie. "I can't sit here and do nothing all day."

"The boutique. We just decided to go."

"Oh, you were talking about today?"

"*Jah.* Never put off today what you can do tomorrow. Wait, maybe that's—"

"The other way around." Elsa-May chuckled and added, "And a little scrambled, but I get the point. I'll just finish this row if you can wait that long."

"Okay, I'll feed Snowy and take him with me when I call for the taxi. I hope he doesn't bark again."

"He'll be okay."

"She said it was the Winston hotel. I believe that's the posh one that opened last year."

"*Jah,* that was the one."

CHAPTER 19

ETTIE AND ELSA-MAY had the taxi take them to the Winston hotel. When they stepped onto the pavement across the road, Ettie looked up at it. "It's some hotel."

"It looks quite grand."

"It does, and so do the shops underneath it. I can't see a dress shop, though."

"It might be actually inside the hotel, like inside the doors. That's the impression I got," Elsa-May said. "After you."

Ettie raised her eyebrows at her sister, but since it had been her idea she had to be the one to go first. When no cars were in sight, she walked across the road followed closely by Elsa-May. When they approached the doors of the hotel, they were opened by a doorman, who gave them a big smile. They thanked him and walked through the doors into a huge lobby. To their left was a large brightly-lit reception desk, and to their right was a large seating area with potted palms beside groupings of armchairs and low tables. Large columns going right to the ceiling were a feature. Straight ahead was a walkway that led to small shops.

"What did I say?" Elsa-May asked.

"Okay." Ettie inhaled deeply and she took another step. Part of her didn't want Tiffany to be at her store today because she had no idea what to say. Another part of her was hoping she would be there so they might find more information.

They looked in the window of the first dress shop they came to. There was a small blonde-haired woman with her hair pulled back into a short ponytail at the nape of her neck.

"That's her," Elsa-May whispered.

"I know." Ettie gulped, and sent up a quick prayer and walked in the door.

Tiffany spun around and continued to adjust a dress on a hanger. She stared at them, looking quite surprised.

"Hello. You're Mrs. Carter, aren't you?"

She smiled without letting it reach her eyes and looked from Ettie to Elsa-May. "You were at my husband's funeral."

"That's right."

Her perfectly shaped pencil-thin eyebrows lowered slightly. "You were sitting with Sparkle."

"Yes. I'm Ettie and this is my sister, Elsa-May. I'm Sparkle's mother."

"Oh." Her jaw dropped open. "Then you'll need to leave."

"Why's that?"

"You're not welcome here."

Elsa-May said, "We were just saying hello." Ettie nodded and then there was an awkward silence, before Elsa-May spoke again. "We were walking by and I said to Ettie, isn't that Mrs. Carter?"

Ettie added, "And I said, you're right it is."

"We're dreadfully sorry about your husband," Elsa-May said.

"Under the circumstances, I don't think I should speak to you and I still can't believe that Sparkle dared to show up at my husband's funeral."

"What makes you think my daughter had something to do with Ian's death?"

There was a noise coming from the back and then a man walked out with an armful of clothing. It was Angelo, Ettie was certain. But he was the son from the first marriage. He looked up at them, shocked.

"I really think you should go," Tiffany said.

"Yes, we're going."

"Were you spying on us?" Tiffany asked, taking a small step toward them.

"No."

"Come on, Ettie." Elsa-May put her hand lightly on Ettie's shoulder and they both walked out of the shop.

"Well, that was about the most embarrassing moment of my life," Ettie said.

"Correct me if I'm wrong, but wasn't that the son from the first marriage? The one who met Myra first?"

Ettie nodded. "That's what I thought. How odd that he'd be in the store with Tiffany as though he were helping her out."

"Does he work for her?"

"No one said anything. From all accounts I thought their relationship, or the relationships between the two wives and each other's sons, was strained. That explains what I saw at the funeral, though. I saw them smiling at each other as though they were friendly. But I'm pretty sure someone told us that Angelo and his half-brother both work at the business Ian had owned and then sold."

"Well, Ettie, we could well have found the clue we were looking for. We might have, we just have to figure out what it means. Let's visit Alice. Isn't it Thursday? The day her employer goes away to play cards?"

Ettie shook her head. "It's not Thursday, but we should go anyway. She might be able to enlighten us about what we just saw and her employer might spare her for a moment or two to talk with us."

Elsa-May pulled a face. "We're not going to tell her, are we?"

"No, but we can ask her some general questions."

"*Jah,* good idea."

As they approached the hotel entrance, the doorman opened the doors and they stepped through.

They found a bus seat a little ways down the sidewalk, and sat down to talk.

"Could the two of them be in it together, Ettie?"

"The second wife and the stepson?"

"*Jah.*"

Ettie thought for a moment. "You would think they wouldn't risk being seen together if they'd conspired to kill Ian and frame Myra."

"Still, it was unexpected that we came across them. Maybe they figured no one with any connection to the case would come into the shop."

Ettie shook her head. "You're wrong. Detective Kelly could've stopped by to ask her questions, or to give her an update."

"Hmm. You might be right. Did Myra think they were friendly with one another—Tiffany and Angelo?"

"Myra didn't think they were. I'm certain that's what she said."

Elsa-May rubbed her chin. "*Jah,* but let's not mention this outing to Myra. We'd have to tell her where we saw them together. She won't be too happy with us if she hears we were at the boutique."

"Why don't we talk with our friend again? I think that's our best next move."

"Alice?" Elsa-May asked.

"*Jah*, and if we don't get the information from her, we'll have to ask Myra how close the two of them were. And, if Angelo had ever been in her house and had an opportunity to plant the poison."

"Good thinking."

Ettie smiled, pleased to get a compliment from her sister, but she couldn't enjoy it for long because Elsa-May was already on her feet.

"Are we going to Alice's now?"

"*Jah.* Like we discussed earlier."

Less than an hour later they were across town, and Ettie and Elsa-May stood outside the house where Alice worked. Elsa-May had her hand out ready to knock on the door when it was flung open. Ettie and Elsa-May were relieved to see Alice standing there rather than her employer.

"What a nice surprise. I saw the two of you get out of the taxi from my bedroom window."

"I hope you don't mind us stopping by, but Ettie and I just have a couple of questions."

"Mrs. Marlborough is out for a time and she won't be home until about five. It's safe enough to come in." Alice stepped back and opened the door wider.

As Ettie stepped through, she asked, "There's no Mr. Marlborough?"

"Yes. He's sick upstairs. He's bedridden. Nurses come in and out to tend to him. He's had his medication and he'll be asleep for hours. Don't worry, he's as deaf as a post and he wouldn't hear us anyway." Alice showed Ettie and Elsa-May into the sitting room. She sat herself down and said, "What is it you want to ask me?"

Elsa-May cleared her throat and then looked at Ettie who was sitting next to her.

Ettie said, "We were just wondering, what is the relationship between Ian Carter's ex-wives and the sons?"

Alice blinked rapidly. "Oh! Since I've been away from that house I haven't had any contact with them."

Elsa-May said, "Plenty of windows overlook the street, so you would see the comings and goings of the Carter household."

"I can tell you they've had Angelo and Maria to the house on a few occasions in the last couple of years. Then for a while, Angelo was often at the house, but not lately. He hasn't been to the house for months. Well, not the house here, but next door."

Elsa-May nodded. "Yes, we know what you mean."

"That annoyed Maria."

"Oh?" Ettie said.

"That would've upset her. She would've been all right about it on the surface, but inside it would have been eating away at her. When Maria first got divorced she was okay about Angelo going over to the house. He was only a boy back then and Maria had her social life, and needed a babysitter I'd dare say. I was working there at that time. He formed a bond with his stepmother, but then his mother, Maria, pulled him away when she saw them getting close."

"Are we talking many years ago?"

"Yes. He was only a boy."

Ettie knew that the bond must still be there.

"We heard you were left stamps," Elsa-May said.

"Yes, and I don't mind saying I was mightily disappointed. After all the time that I spent with that family would expect a little more even though the second wife never liked me.

"I'm sorry to hear that."

Alice shrugged her bony shoulders. "It doesn't matter. Not really."

Ettie said, "My daughter and Ian were good friends, as I mentioned before, but what I didn't know last time I saw you, was that he left her a valuable diamond. It was in its crystal formation, and she had no idea it was in his collection until after she'd been given it in his will. She was pleased that he left her his crystal collection, but it was so much more than that."

"That would've been a lovely surprise for her."

Ettie licked her lips. "I wouldn't be surprised if one of those stamps he gave you might be very valuable."

Alice's face brightened and she straightened up. "Do you think so?"

Elsa-May gasped. "Oh, Ettie. You shouldn't get her hopes up like that."

"I was completely ignored, Elsa-May, when I went to the reading of the will. Sparkle smiled at me and I hadn't even met her before that. Neither of the wives or the sons acknowledged me. It hurt me to be treated like that." Alice grinned. "I'd like the stamps to be valuable and that'd show 'em. Do you really think they might be of some value, Ettie?"

Bearing in mind what Elsa-May said, she downplayed it slightly. "You never know. It doesn't hurt to find out."

"Very well. If you say so. I will take them to a stamp appraiser. I know a man in town who knows about stamps. He sells them."

"That sounds like a good place to start," Ettie said.

"I don't know a thing about stamps except you need to put one on a letter before you put it in the mailbox." Alice giggled.

"Don't get your hopes up too much because the detective was the one who found out about the valuable diamond in the crystal collection. Surely if one of those stamps was of great value the lawyer would've known about it and would've informed the detective."

"Don't worry, Elsa-May, I won't get my hopes up. It doesn't hurt to check though, does it?"

Elsa-May shook her head.

"I'm going to take a whole day off tomorrow and have my stamps looked at."

"I hope you find it's good news," Ettie said. "Thanks for telling us what you know about the Carters."

"We wouldn't mind talking to Maria. Do you know how we can do that?" Elsa-May asked. "Does she work?"

"She doesn't have a paid job. She's a volunteer at the local hospital down the road."

"Really?"

"I told you she was a nice woman. She wouldn't have made up a story about me stealing like Ian's second wife did."

"What exactly were you accused of stealing?" Ettie asked.

"Some of the silverware. Pieces of a solid silver tea set went missing and it wasn't me. I didn't even know it was solid silver until they had to put in the insurance claim."

Elsa-May rose to her feet. "Thank you, Alice."

When Ettie stood as well, she said, "Would you happen to know what days Maria works at the hospital?"

"She seems to be there all the time. I know that because Mr. Marlborough often has to go there for blood transfusions and I always see her."

They thanked Alice once more and asked her if she wouldn't mind calling them a taxi.

Once Ettie and Elsa-May were in the taxi heading to the hospital, Elsa-May said, "Why did you tell her that about the stamps? She'll be bitterly disappointed."

"Let's talk about that later. Right now, why are we going to the hospital?"

"Have you got anything wrong with you?" Elsa-May asked.

Ettie frowned. *"Nee,* of course not!"

"I've been a bit dizzy lately."

"Have you? You haven't mentioned it?"

Elsa-May grinned. "It wouldn't hurt to get it checked out."

"I don't know why you didn't tell me before now. It could be something serious like your blood pressure or something."

"We'll soon see," Elsa-May said.

Once the taxi let them out in front of the hospital, they made their way to the emergency and outpatients area. The lady behind the reception desk had Elsa-May take a seat after handing her a bunch of forms to fill out.

"I'm quite worried about your episodes and I don't know why you didn't say anything sooner."

Elsa-May kept her head down filling in the forms. "I didn't want to worry you."

"You worry me more knowing you didn't get it checked."

"Stop fussing, Ettie. This is why I didn't say anything. Where would we find Maria," Elsa-May whispered.

"Would she work on the wards?" Ettie looked around. "She probably wouldn't work in this area of the hospital."

"I don't know, perhaps we'll have to check on all the floors when it's visiting hours."

Ettie sighed.

"What's wrong now?" Elsa-May looked at Ettie.

"I don't think volunteers are going to hang around at visiting hours."

All of a sudden, Ettie dug Elsa-May in the ribs.

"Ow! What was that for?" Elsa-May rubbed her side and the pen fell from her hand onto the floor.

"Your teddy bears. Ask to talk to one of the volunteers about the group of ladies who are making the teddy bears."

"Brilliant idea, Ettie!"

"Really?" Ettie leaned down and picked up the pen and handed it to Elsa-May.

"Jah." Elsa-May took the pen and placed it on the spare chair beside her. "And now I don't need to get my dizzy spells checked."

Ettie pulled Elsa-May back down when she was trying to get up. "You do have to get your dizzy spells checked."

"Oh, wake up and smell the coffee, Ettie. I don't have dizzy spells at all and never have."

"You don't?"

"Nee. Well, maybe if I'm sitting for awhile and stand up quickly."

"You were just making it all up?"

"Don't make me feel bad. It was a slight exaggeration so we could get into the hospital and close to Maria. Why couldn't you have come up with the teddy bear idea in the taxi on the way over?"

Ettie shrugged. "Why didn't you?"

Elsa-May stood and ripped up the forms and threw them in a nearby trash can. Then she made her way back to Ettie. "We need to go to the main reception area of the hospital and ask to speak to one of the volunteers."

"Why don't you ask for Maria by name?"

"Ettie you're a—"

"Genius?"

Elsa-May lips downturned. "I wouldn't go that far."

"It was another good idea though, wasn't it?"

"*Jah,* it was."

CHAPTER 20

WHEN THEY FOUND the hospital's central reception, they spoke to the woman behind the desk and told her they needed to speak with Maria. When it didn't look like they were getting anywhere, Elsa-May mentioned the teddy bears. Then they found out Maria was in charge of all the volunteers, so she would've been the right person to speak to anyway. The receptionist picked up the phone and spoke to Maria and then hung up the phone.

"If you go up to level three in the elevator, she'll be waiting in the office directly opposite."

Together they made their way up in the elevator.

"I can't believe this has all been so easy," Ettie said.

"We just have to somehow bring the conversation around to the Carters."

When the elevator doors opened they headed to the office ahead of them and walked in through the open door. Maria got up from behind a desk and walked over with a big smile, her right arm extended to shake their hands. "Hello. You look familiar. Were you at Ian's funeral?"

"That's right. I'm Elsa-May, and this is my sister, Ettie. Ettie is Sparkle's mother."

Maria frowned. "I'm sorry?"

Ettie said, "Sparkle was a friend of Ian's. She is a healer of sorts."

"Ah, I imagine that is some new age thing. I'm sorry I don't know anyone by the name Sparkle."

"That's right," Ettie said.

"Have a seat."

They all sat and Elsa-May proceeded to tell Maria about the ladies' group and knitting the teddy bears.

"I can't tell you what smiles come to the patients' faces when they're given a teddy bear. And I'm telling you, it's not just the young. Everybody loves them. And if you can provide us with hand knitted ones that'll make it even more special. We used to have the knitted teddy bears years ago, I'm sure we did. We'd be delighted to have them again."

Elsa-May smiled and Ettie said, "It was Alice, the housekeeper, who told us you were here. We were wondering how to get the teddy bears into the hospitals."

"I haven't seen Alice for years until I saw her the other day. I wanted to ask her how she was, but it was neither the time nor the place, I'm afraid. Did she mention it to you? I've been upset about the fact that I didn't talk to her. It was at the reading of Ian's will. I know how easily she gets upset."

"How so?" asked Elsa-May.

"She's a sensitive soul. She's the kind of person who gets easily offended. And the other day, I'm afraid a little family politics was involved. I didn't want the other side to know that I was still on good terms with her. I suppose you know that Ian's second wife wanted her fired?"

"We heard something about that."

"It was silly really. All over her taking a few stamps."

Elsa-May said, "Don't you mean items of silverware?"

"Oh no, it was definitely stamps. Ian used to buy and sell stamps on the side and some of them were quite rare and valuable. He must've sold most of them because I happen to know there were only a few stamps given to Alice."

"So, you don't think they were very valuable?"

"I know there was one that I thought Ian would never sell. He must've, though."

"Why do you say that?" Ettie asked.

"Because there were no stamps left in the will except the stamps given to the housekeeper." Maria laughed. "I don't know why I'm telling you all this. I never tell anyone anything about my private business."

"We won't let it go further," Elsa-May said with a sincere smile.

Ettie didn't say any more about the stamps and neither did Elsa-May.

"Forgive me for asking, but how do you and your son get along with Tiffany?" Elsa-May asked.

"Civil at times, most of the time we try to be. As civil I can be to someone who deliberately set out to trap my husband."

"I'm sorry to hear that," Ettie said.

"Yes, it was rather traumatic at the time, but I'm over it now. It was years ago. Time heals all wounds they say and I've found that to be true."

"My daughter, Sparkle, knew Ian and your son too. They both came to her for crystal healing, or some such thing."

"Angelo has very different ideas from me. I don't go in for all that kind of thing."

"It's too weird for us too," Elsa-May said.

Maria nodded. "At least Ian listened to Angelo about things like that. Angelo would come up with all these weird ideas and Ian would follow him. Anyway, enough about me and my family. When shall we expect those teddies?"

"Can we take your phone number? Then I'll speak to the ladies in the group and we'll estimate when the first batch will be ready."

"That will be wonderful." She stood up and pulled two flyers out of her desk. "Have a cup of complimentary coffee before you leave the hospital. The cafeteria is on the first floor."

"Thank you. That's very nice of you," Ettie said.

Elsa-May leaned forward and took hold of the flyers. "Thank you. We could each do with a cup of coffee right now."

"Good. And here's my card with the phone number. I'll be looking forward to hearing from you."

As THEY HEADED to the cafeteria, Ettie whispered, "That went well. Better than I thought it would."

"*Jah,* it did."

"Then why are you looking so worried?"

"She said a cup of complimentary coffee, but she should've said, in my mind, a complimentary cup of coffee."

Ettie scoffed. "You're just impossible, Elsa-May. Either way we're getting free coffee."

Elsa-May chuckled. "I suppose you're right. I wasn't worried, I was just going over the options of the word placement, wondering which it should've been."

Soon, they were sitting down with their cups of coffee, looking out onto the courtyard of the cafeteria.

"Let's go over what we know so far," Elsa-May said.

"I hope you're not stepping on Michelle's toes regarding the teddies. She was the one in charge of the teddy distribution, wasn't she?"

"I don't see that as a problem. I've saved her lot of work. I hope so. Anyway, so far, you might be right about the stamps. One of those could very well be valuable. Were you listening when she said that Ian had owned a valuable one?"

Ettie nodded. "What if Alice knew there was a valuable stamp left in his collection? The one that he'd never sell?"

"She didn't say so."

Ettie shook her head. *"Nee,* she didn't say so."

"If she knew about the stamp collection, she was doing a very good job covering it up when she spoke to us."

"We both know Myra didn't do it, so who are our suspect so far?" Ettie asked.

"Maria could have done it out of revenge, but she wasn't the one who put the blame on Myra, right?"

"I don't know. That seems to be true. We've been focusing on Tiffany as the accuser, figuring she's the killer."

Elsa-May took a sip of her coffee. *"Jah,* there's Tiffany, who should inherit most of the money. She had the biggest motive."

Ettie shook her head. "That doesn't fit. She could've done it at any time in any other way so why wait until now to kill him? Then again, she did make up that story about Myra, It had to be Tiffany and she could've been involved in the murder with her stepson. And the stepson had access to Myra's house."

"One thing puzzles me though, Ettie."

"And what's that?"

"It's about the stamps."

"Jah, I've been worried about that as well. She told us she'd been accused of stealing silverware and not stamps. Maria had no reason to lie to us about that. The question is—"

"Why did Alice lie to us?"

"That's exactly what I was going to say before you interrupted." Ettie stared into her coffee.

"Do you think we should pay Alice another visit and ask her whether it was silverware or stamps that she was accused of stealing, and ask her why she lied to us?"

Ettie pressed her lips together. "It seems a petty thing to ask."

"I know, but I think it's the only way we can get to the bottom of things. At the very least she might tell us some more information."

"It's worth a try. And we should leave soon so we get there before Mrs. Marlborough gets home." Ettie stood and smoothed down her dress and then heard Elsa-May slurp her coffee loudly. She was glad that there was barely anyone else in the cafeteria to hear her sister's display of poor table manners.

CHAPTER 21

WHEN THEY ARRIVED at the Marlborough home, they saw bags being piled into a taxi and then Alice came bustling out of the house. They had their taxi driver wait while they talked to Alice.

"Are you going somewhere, Alice?" Elsa-May asked.

Alice didn't look pleased to see them, not at all.

"Alice, we haven't said anything to anyone yet, but we know you killed Ian." Ettie didn't know that, but she took a wild guess and was glad that Elsa-May remained silent except for a quick little gasp.

Alice blew out a breath. "How did you figure it out?"

"It was the lie about the stamps and the silverware."

Alice hung her head. "It's true. I couldn't wait any longer for my stamp. It was supposed to be for my retirement and Mr. Carter was taking too long to die. I wasn't paid enough by Ian or his parents, so I never had enough

159

to save for my retirement and, because I constantly worked in the home, I never met a man and I couldn't get married. Ian and his family owed me that much."

"You knew he was leaving you the stamp collection?" Elsa-May asked.

"Yes. He told me. He told me on the day that Tiffany made him terminate my employment. I was relieved to know I was going to have something in my old age. We both knew he didn't have long to live. He surprised us all by living as long as he did. He'd already lived long enough back then."

"Long enough?" Ettie asked.

"He had outlived the doctor's expectations."

"Where did you obtain the poison?" Elsa-May asked.

"More importantly, why did you put it in Myra's house?"

"I didn't put it in anybody's house. When I told Angelo what I was planning on doing—"

"Angelo was in on this?"

"He didn't kill his father, I killed Ian."

"Who put it in Myra's house?"

"Angelo did it. And he came up with the plan and got the poison."

Elsa-May trembled. "Who put the poison on the crystals?"

"Angelo did it at a special laboratory, but it was my idea to kill Ian to get the stamp. I can't work for too much longer. I'm an old woman. Now, at least I've got something. I worked for it."

Ettie looked down at the floor. "I thought Angelo and Myra got along well."

"I'm sorry, Ettie. I didn't know you back then and didn't know your daughter. Angelo said it was best to have the police suspect someone and he suggested a woman called Sparkle. He said there was some kind of meeting going on at her house and it would be a perfect time to plant the poison. I just went along with his suggestion. I didn't want to get caught. Oh dear, I guess you're going to tell the police and then I'll go to jail."

"Or worse," Elsa-May said.

"I do have a second cousin in England."

"You're thinking of fleeing the country?" Ettie asked glancing at the waiting taxi and the driver who was now in the car.

"I think I have to. I don't know what prompted me to get a passport a few years ago, but I'm awfully glad I did. Now, if you'll excuse me."

"Can you confess first, please, so my daughter doesn't go to jail?"

"All right I will. I'll send a full confession to the detective once I'm well and truly clear and out of the county. So, excuse me, but I've got some driving to do." She got into the front passenger side of the taxi.

Ettie and Elsa-May stood staring at the taxi,

watching it get smaller and smaller as she disappeared into the distance.

"That's the last we'll see of her. I hope Detective Kelly believes us and I hope she does make the time to write that full confession."

"Where do you think she's going now?" Ettie asked.

"My guess is to the nearest airport. She has that postage stamp somewhere on her person and she won't be making any stops. Mark my words, she is headed to the nearest airport."

"We have to tell Kelly."

"Why? She could hang," Elsa-May said.

"They don't hang people these days."

"You know what I mean. They still have the death penalty."

Ettie touched her head, feeling a massive headache coming on. "We need to tell Kelly because of Myra."

"It's not our way to interfere in these things, Ettie."

"Oh, now you don't want to interfere? You interfere with everything all the time."

"Okay, I'll come with you. I suppose I shouldn't have said that."

The two ladies had the taxi take them to the station. On the way, they told the driver they had an emergency and he allowed them to use his cell phone. Ettie called Detective Kelly's cell phone. When he answered on the second ring, she told him everything that Alice had said. He thanked her and hung up quickly.

"He believed you?" Elsa-May asked.

"He didn't say he didn't."

"That's a good sign."

Ettie had the taxi take them to the bottom of their street and then they walked slowly back to the house in silence. Ettie knew that Elsa-May was feeling slightly sorry for Alice. It was a fearful thing to be old and faced with the prospect of no money, nowhere to live, and an uncertain future. Alice killed a man who was already dying and killed out of fear of her future. Even though nothing could excuse taking someone's life, Ettie could see how Alice had justified herself in doing so.

CHAPTER 22

THE NEXT DAY, Kelly knocked on Ettie and Elsa-May's door. As Elsa-May pushed Snowy into one of the bedrooms, Ettie ushered Kelly into the living room. They were both eager to hear what he had to say.

"Alice managed to slip through our fingers, but we have arrested Angelo. What he's confessed so far sounds like he might have been the mastermind."

"And what about what Tiffany said about Myra?" Ettie asked.

Kelly glanced at his wristwatch. "She's coming into the station at six for questioning. Angelo is remaining tight-lipped over her involvement but I'm sure if we apply a little pressure on him he'll cave. Or maybe seeing the trouble he's in will prompt her to confess her part in all of it."

"Ettie and I saw Angelo at her boutique."

His eyebrows rose. "At Tiffany's boutique in the Winston?"

"Yes."

"You were shopping there?"

"Walking by," Ettie said.

He shook his head. "That is interesting information."

Elsa-May interlaced her fingers together. "He was coming out of the back room with clothes over his arm and looking like he worked there."

"That's good to know. Thank you. We'll wait and see what happens. The next twenty-four hours should be very interesting. What you've told me just now falls in line with the information we've found out."

Elsa-May leaned forward. "And what's that?"

"If you keep it to yourselves, I can tell you that there was a sizeable sum withdrawn from Tiffany's account not long before Ian died."

"A payoff?" Elsa-May asked.

"Could be."

"I've given this a lot of thought since we talked to Alice," said Ettie, "and this is my theory. Angelo was friendly with his old housekeeper, we all know that now. Alice told him what she was planning and Angelo agreed to help. After all, he was waiting on the old man to die too."

"Go on," Kelly said.

"Then he told his stepmother his plan, leaving out

Alice's involvement. After all, Alice had only told him she wanted Ian dead. The rest of the plan must've been Angelo's because Alice knew nothing about Myra except there was to be a scapegoat. It was he who sourced the poison and leaned how to safely apply it, and he made sure his father died after coming into contact with it. It was Angelo who placed the poison in Myra's house, in a place she'd never find it, possibly long before Ian died."

Kelly crossed one leg over the other. "So, you're saying that you think Angelo approached his step-mother with a plan and she paid him to carry it out? Not knowing he was going to do it anyway?"

"Yes. You said it so much better."

Kelly slowly nodded. "That makes sense and that's the conclusion I'd come to as well."

"Oh, I'm so glad that Myra's in the clear."

"Me too. I don't like arresting the wrong person for a crime such as this. I must say, I missed this one in the beginning. Who would've thought that the son— Ian's first son would have been in on it with the former housekeeper?"

"Ettie did," Elsa-May said.

He looked at Ettie. "What was it that led you to the housekeeper?"

"We talked to her about the family, and she lied to us about the silverware."

"Silverware?"

Elsa-May explained, "She told us Tiffany concocted

a story about her stealing silverware, when really it was stamps."

"How did you find out … Forget it. How did you meet … Forget it." He shook his head.

"She knew she was being left a valuable stamp and that's why she hurried his death along. That's what she told us before she rode away in the taxi."

"I know that now. You could put yourselves in dangerous situations doing what you did."

"We had to do something because I couldn't see my daughter go to jail for something she didn't do."

He nodded. "I understand. I understand that very well. And if I had been in your situation, I would've done all I could, too. Sadly, I've never had children of my own. I'm sorry I had to arrest her, but you must understand how the evidence looked."

Ettie ignored him and then they all jumped when there was a sudden loud knock on the door.

"I think this might be Myra." Ettie pushed herself off her chair and hurried to the door. There before her was the angry man from next door.

"Your bloomin' dang dog was barking again all day."

"I think that's an exaggeration. Your wife told us that he only barked once or twice the other day. He's really not a barker."

"If you can't shut him up, I'll call the police and have him put down."

"Did you say you need the police?" Kelly appeared at Ettie's side. "How can I help you?"

"Ah…" the man's eyes went wide as he took a step back, and Kelly instantly took a matching step forward.

"Did you want to make an official complaint against these two elderly widows and their harmless canine companion? We're not in the habit of killing dogs for barking."

Greville stepped back again until he was nearly to the edge of the porch. "No, there's no problem really. My wife just gets headaches and she's very sensitive to noise."

Detective Kelly said, "I'm Detective Kelly. I didn't catch your name."

"Greville."

"Greville …?"

"Greville Charmers."

Kelly nodded to him. "Good evening, Mr. Charmers."

"Yes, good night." Greville turned and left.

The detective stepped back inside and Ettie closed the door. "Thank you."

Kelly chuckled. "I think he's very nervous when it comes to the police."

"Seems like it," Elsa-May said with a chuckle.

Ettie giggled. "I don't think we'll be having any problem with him anymore."

"If you do, let me know. I should go. I've got that interview at six and after that I've got a mountain of paperwork waiting for me."

"Thanks for letting us know what's happening."

"No problem. Maybe next time I stop by you might offer me cake?"

Ettie said, "We have cake. I'll put the kettle on, if you have the time?"

He chuckled. "Thank you, but I don't today. I must go. I was teasing you."

"Oh."

When Kelly left, Elsa-May let Snowy out of the bedroom and they settled down for a quiet dinner.

CHAPTER 23

THAT NIGHT, they heard nothing from Myra. It wasn't until the following night that she came to their door.

Ettie opened the door to see her daughter in another of her flowing kaftans. This time, it was primarily pink and orange. Instead of her hair being piled on top of her head, it was flowing about her shoulders. She stepped inside without saying a word and Ettie closed the door behind her.

Elsa-May looked up from knitting the first of many teddy bears. "Hello, Sparkle."

Snowy was in his bed, and he lifted his head.

"Hello, Snowy." She sat and slapped her knees calling Snowy. Slowly he got off his bed and put his front paws on Myra's legs.

"Snowy doesn't jump," Elsa-May said.

"He doesn't?"

"No. You have to pick him up." Ettie said as she bent

down, picked up Snowy and placed him on Myra's lap. Snowy quickly settled down on Myra's lap and placed his head between his paws.

"What a sweet little dog."

Elsa-May chortled. "Not according to our new neighbors. They've been complaining that he barks."

"And does he?"

"I'm sure he doesn't."

Ettie sat on the couch next to Myra.

Myra stroked Snowy. "I've come here to say thanks for your help, Mother. I knew you be up for it."

Ettie put an arm around her daughter's shoulder. "I told you everything would work out."

"And you're right. However did you figure it out, that it was the previous housekeeper and Angelo, and Tiffany as well?"

"Tiffany?" Elsa-May and Ettie looked at one another.

"Yes, she's been arrested."

"We didn't know that part," Ettie said. "Kelly was here yesterday and said she was coming in for questioning, but we didn't know for sure she was involved. Although, going by what you said, she had to be involved somewhere."

"Yes, she would've been better off keeping her mouth closed and not trying to implicate me."

Ettie nodded. "And how did they get that poison into your house?"

"Angelo finally admitted putting it there. He often

came to the house for different functions and seminars that I held."

"That explains that. And Ronald?" Elsa-May asked leaning forward.

"He's fine. He was very upset with me for keeping it all from him. Kelly told him what was happening, and he came back right away."

"What about that case he was working on?"

"He said it had come to a dead end anyway." Myra shrugged her shoulders. "I don't know if maybe he told me that just to make me feel better."

Elsa-May leaned forward. "Don't you feel so much better now that he's back?"

Myra smiled and nodded. "I do."

"Do you think we'll hear wedding bells any time soon?" Elsa-May asked.

"Weddings are such an outdated experience and marriage is just a piece of paper."

"It's much more than that. Vows are made before God," Elsa-May said.

"Anyway, Ronald is set in his ways. We're happy as we are. He has his house and I have mine. We're always there for one another. It's a good arrangement for both of us."

Elsa-May nodded. "As long as you're happy, I suppose."

"Mother, I know you'll only be happy if I come back to the community."

"That's not so. You have your own choice to make and I respect that."

"Do you, Mother?"

"Well, of course I'd like it if things were a little different."

"I knew it."

"Don't be so hard on your *mudder*," Elsa-May said.

"I'm not hard on her. I'm not hard on her at all." She turned to Ettie. "I'm grateful that you're always here when I'm in trouble, Mom."

Ettie looked into her daughter's eyes and saw sincerity. She hadn't called her Mom or even *Mamm* for years. Ettie could barely keep the smile from her face. "I'm glad that you came to me."

"Now where is that cup of hot tea?"

"Your mother got you some green tea when we were at the markets."

Myra's face lit up. "Did you?"

"*Jah.*"

"I might have to visit a little more often."

"I wouldn't mind that a bit," Ettie said. "In fact, it would be a pleasure."

After Myra left their house, Ettie and Elsa-May decided to sit for a moment in the living room before they went to bed.

"It's a funny world, Elsa-May."

"It can be, *jah,* but what do you mean in particular?"

"Look how different Myra and I are. Who does she take after, being so different from me?"

Elsa-May frowned. "Does she have to take after anyone?"

"I suppose not, but people usually do, don't they?"

"Hmm. I think she's a lot like you."

Ettie giggled. "Me?"

"Jah. Both you and Myra see things differently than other people."

"I'm not out there trying to heal people with crystals and whatever else she does."

"Nee, but you have the ability to look at things differently from most people, and that seems to be what Myra does."

"We're both strange. That's what you're saying."

Elsa-May smiled. "I could've said that, but I didn't."

Ettie sighed. "You might be right. I don't know what her *vadder* would say if he were alive to see her now."

"She's not doing too bad."

"But she's not in the community."

"There's still time," Elsa-May said. "You never know what the future holds."

"Do you think these experiences she's having will lead her back one day?"

"Only *Gott* knows that, Ettie, but it's not out of the realms of possibility. Miracles do happen."

Ettie reached out to the other end of the couch and patted Snowy. *"Jah* they do."

"It seems you were right about how it all happened, Ettie."

"I'd say so."

"Aren't you surprised?"

Ettie shook her head. *"Nee.* How are you getting along with your teddy bear?"

Elsa-May reached down and picked up her knitting. All Ettie saw was a brown square. "Hmm. It doesn't look like much now, but it will look like a teddy when it's finished."

"I hope so for the sake of the children."

"This teddy will be going to the hospital where Maria works."

Ettie shook her head. "And what do you think Michelle will say when you tell her the teddies aren't going to the Children's Hospital?"

"I'm sure Maria's hospital has children go there, so they will be bringing smiles to children's faces as well."

"Hmm. You told me she wanted them to go to the Children's Hospital."

"I've given that some thought. If she doesn't like it, I'll make all the teddies for Maria's hospital myself."

Ettie giggled.

"What's so funny?"

"Nothing."

"Well, it must be something."

"I just thought how busy you're going to be knitting."

"Why's that?"

"Ava's *boppli.*"

Elsa-May let the teddy bear she was knitting drop into her lap. "I didn't think of that. I must start knitting for the new arrival, and don't forget we've got to go to Ava's *haus* for dinner soon."

"I won't forget." Ettie's jaw dropped open. "What about Maria and the hospital expecting all the—"

"I don't know. I'll have to do it all somehow. I'll have to supply a whole hospital with bears and I can't knit less for the new *boppli* than I have for the others."

Elsa-May looked so worried that Ettie said, "Why don't I give you a hand?"

Elsa-May stared at Ettie with her piercing blue eyes. "Would you?"

"I think I can put my needlework aside and we can work on your two projects together."

"Denke, Ettie."

"I've been thinking about Ian."

"And?"

"He really didn't get along with either son. He divorced his first wife and didn't get along with the second. It's sad, don't you think?"

"It is."

"He had Myra as a friend. No wonder he stayed after his sessions with her just to talk. And, funniest thing of all is that Alice has gone to England and can't be found. She got away with it."

"For now." Elsa-May yawned. "That's enough for me. Another day is over."

"I appreciate you, Elsa-May."

Elsa-May frowned. "What are you going on about now?"

"I mean it. We've always had one another and sometimes you're annoying and irritating, but you're always there when I need you, and we help each other."

"Is that why you agreed to knit the teddies?"

"Maybe."

While Elsa-May leaned down to pack her knitting away, she said, "I'll take it."

"Take what?"

"The offer to knit the teddies no matter what the reason."

Ettie chuckled. *"Gut nacht."*

"Gut nacht." Elsa-May headed off to bed and Snowy looked up from his dog bed and scurried after her. Elsa-May poked her head around her bedroom door. "Are we getting a storm?"

"What?"

"You just said we're getting a storm."

Ettie pulled her mouth to one side. "I hope not." Elsa-May was hearing things again.

Elsa-May shook her head at Ettie and closed her bedroom door just as there came a loud knock on the front door.

Ettie jumped, and then rushed to Elsa-May's bedroom and flung open her sister's door. "It might be Granville from next door!"

"Greville," Elsa-May corrected, having yet to even remove her *kapp* in preparation for bed.

"I'm not going to answer the door alone."

"Okay, let's go."

The two sisters walked to the door and at the last instant, Elsa-May pushed Ettie in front so she'd have to open the door. To their immense relief, it was Crowley.

"Hello, you two. I'm sorry about the late hour, but I saw your light on."

"Come in, come in!" Ettie said grabbing hold of his sleeve and pulling him inside.

"We haven't seen you for years." Elsa-May looked him up and down.

He chuckled. "I'm sure it hasn't been that long."

"Do you have time for tea and cake?" Ettie glanced at the clock and saw that it was only seven in the evening. For some reason she'd thought it was much later. Time enough for sharing cake and a pot of hot tea.

His lips turned upward at the corners. "If that's not too much trouble."

"It's not, not at all. Come into the kitchen so you can talk with us while Ettie prepares our snack."

Crowley followed Elsa-May into the kitchen. As soon as he was seated, Elsa-May sat down opposite him. "Now, how are you and Sparkle getting along?"

"Oh, Elsa-May. Do you have to call her that name?" Ettie asked.

Crowley chuckled and cleared his throat. "We're doing great. I know we seem a bit of an odd couple, but they say opposites attract. Anyway, I'm here to thank you both for getting Sparkle out of the scrape she was just in. I can't believe she kept me in the dark about it, but that's the way she is, always mindful of others."

"She's still my daughter, no matter what she does or what she calls herself. I can't say I can agree with all the hocus pocus she goes on with, but she always was different. Sometimes I think she does it to shock me." Ettie filled the teakettle and then popped it onto the stove. Then she got a cake out of its tin, sliced it and placed it on a plate on the center of the table. "We have boiled fruitcake."

"I love that. It'll be a treat; I can't recall the last time I had fruitcake."

"Good. I'm glad that we had one on hand, then."

Crowley reached out and took a piece of cake and had his mouth open to take a bite when Elsa-May said, "What happened with that old case you were working on?"

He lowered his hand. "Ah, that's been a puzzling one. I could never get it out of my head."

"Then you should tell us about it."

"Maybe another day."

"There's no time like the present." Elsa-May bit into a piece of cake.

He shook his head. "It's too late in the day to even begin."

"It's so good to see you again. We've missed you," Ettie said as she scooped tea leaves into a teapot and then added the hot water. "You were never grumpy like Detective Kelly."

He finished chewing his mouthful. "You should feed him more cake. Cakes like this."

Elsa-May raised her eyebrows. "We don't, do we, Ettie?"

"We used to bake for him, and he was nicer back then."

Crowley grinned. "There's nothing like cake to—"

"Soften a grumpy detective's mood?" Elsa-May asked.

"Yes. The job comes with a great deal of pressure, lack of sleep, and a lot of worry. I'm glad I'm out of it."

"Pie didn't work for Greville next door."

The detective leaned forward. "Did you say Greville?"

"I did. That's the name of our new neighbor. His wife seems lovely, but he's mean and he doesn't like dogs." Elsa-May looked around. "Where is Snowy, Ettie?"

"He followed you to your room."

"Oh. He must have stayed there and gone to sleep."

LATER THAT NIGHT, when Crowley had gone home and Elsa-May and Snowy were in bed, Ettie turned the lights off and peered out the kitchen window where she had a good view of the neighbors' house. All the lights were out, from what she could tell, except in the living room. She could see they had a TV on. That was all she could see between the blinds.

Ettie shrugged off the thoughts about the odd neighbors and was left alone to ponder her life. She'd raised many *kinner* and all had stayed in the community but two. She'd had a good marriage to a man she was in love with and she had many friends. Closing her eyes, she said a silent prayer of thanks for her life and wondered how long she had left. At her age, she was thankful for each and every day.

"What do you have in store for me next?" she said out aloud to God.

Thank you for reading Old Promises.

THE NEXT BOOK IN THE SERIES

Book 16
Amish Mystery at Rose Cottage

Widow Nell is consumed by an unresolved mystery from her past—Jedidiah Shoneberger, an Amish man who vanished without a trace over forty years ago, mere weeks before their wedding. Overwhelmed by a mix of grief and lingering affection, she reaches out to Ettie Smith for assistance in piecing together the puzzle of Jedidiah's disappearance.

Faced with the challenge of a cold case, Ettie finds an unexpected ally in her willful older sister, drawing them both into a maze of hidden truths and well-crafted deception. As they pick apart the past, they uncover a shocking detail: Jedidiah wasn't the only one who evaporated into thin air all those years ago. Could Jedidiah be somewhere out there, shrouded in

the mists of time? And who was the cryptic man Nell recalls having heated exchanges with Jedidiah on multiple occasions? Each mystery they unearth seems to guide them back to the serene Rose Cottage. What secrets does this seemingly tranquil dwelling hold?
As Ettie and her sister dig deeper, they must grapple with the idea that some truths are concealed for a reason. With each door they unlock, they risk stirring a past that was meant to lie still. Prepare yourself for an intense journey into the core of a decades-old mystery, where the answers are veiled in the quiet whispers of Rose Cottage.

ABOUT SAMANTHA PRICE

Samantha Price is a USA Today bestselling and Kindle All Stars author of Amish romance books and cozy mysteries. She was raised Brethren and has a deep affinity for the Amish way of life, which she has explored extensively with over a decade of research.

She is mother to two pampered rescue cats, and a very spoiled staffy with separation issues.

www.SamanthaPriceAuthor.com

ALL SAMANTHA PRICE BOOK SERIES

Amish Maids Trilogy

Amish Love Blooms

Amish Misfits

The Amish Bonnet Sisters

Amish Women of Pleasant Valley

Ettie Smith Amish Mysteries

Amish Secret Widows' Society

Expectant Amish Widows

Seven Amish Bachelors

Amish Foster Girls

Amish Brides

Amish Romance Secrets

Amish Christmas Books

Amish Wedding Season

ETTIE SMITH AMISH MYSTERIES

Book 18 Fear Thy Neighbor
Book 19 Amish Winter Murder Mystery
Book 20 Amish Scarecrow Murders
Book 21 Threadly Secret
Book 22 Sugar and Spite
Book 23 A Puzzling Amish Murder
Book 24 Amish Dead and Breakfast
Book 25 Amish Mishaps and Murder
Book 26 A Deadly Amish Betrayal
Book 27 Amish Buggy Murder

Made in the USA
Columbia, SC
14 October 2023

24459229R00107